TEAM TRIASSIC

Journeys Ahead

Daniel J. Grimm
with Bonnie W. Goldfein

BALBOA.
PRESS

A DIVISION OF HAY HOUSE

Balboa Press books may be ordered through booksellers or by contacting:

Balboa Press
A Division of Hay House
1663 Liberty Drive
Bloomington, IN 47403
www.balboapress.com
1 (877) 407-4847

Print information available on the last page.

ISBN: 978-1-9822-2373-1 (sc)
ISBN: 978-1-9822-2372-4 (hc)
ISBN: 978-1-9822-2374-8 (e)

Library of Congress Control Number: 2019903006

Balboa Press rev. date: 03/21/2019

Chapter 1

I am lucky to be alive. A little more than a year ago I was in Centennial Hills Hospital, room 617, snoozing away in a deep coma as my body tried to fight off the poison injected into me during my very first one-on-one fight with a dino hybrid.

Until that day, the only dino hybrids I knew were my friends and some other kids at school, and we had only morphed from human to our individual dinosaurs for fun – and always keeping within the Las Vegas city regulations prohibiting full-extension morphing for nearly all hybrids. Dad's "recipe" combining the genomes of a bunch of dinosaurs and other animals had made me what he called a *Regem Insuprabilus* – "unbeatable king" — soon after my birth as a *Velociraptor* hybrid, but I never really knew what size, powers or abilities I would have at full extension. All that changed last September 10th.

On that day, the city of Las Vegas experienced the terror and destruction that a single rogue dinosaur could deliver in only a few hours. After destroying homes in one area of the Northwest section of town, the beast made its way to my Middle School – no one knows why – and nearly killed my friend Nick before I morphed into my *Regem Insuprabilus* dino and managed to fight it off and kill it. My "souvenir" of this battle was the *SpinoRex* poison that kept me comatose for over a month, until Dad developed an antitoxin that saved my life.

Once I woke up, Dad and Mom filled my brother Andy and me in on the "Lone Mountain Project." After a family picnic on the mountain over a year ago, they had shown us a large cleared area on the east side of the mountain. At the time, they were very secretive about just WHY they showed us the land; but when I woke up and they learned just how earnest my friends were about the whole Team Triassic thing, they obviously decided the time was right to let Andy and me in on what was happening.

On the dining room table, Dad unfolded blueprints for a massive structure, over 80,000 square feet divided into three floors of rooms overlooking the city.

"This is our new laboratory," he said, proudly.

I was stunned. How could we afford to build a huge laboratory on Lone Mountain? Dad might be a genius, but most of his work with human-dino hybrids had been in secret... and even if he did research in the open, scientists like him certainly didn't make enough money to build what has to be a multi-million-dollar lab!

"B-bbut... how can we afford... Where did you get... Um, I don't understand..." I sputtered.

Dad winked at Mom as he pulled a letter out of his lab coat pocket.

"This is how," he said, spreading the one-page letter out on the table. It was only three short paragraphs, but its message was crystal-clear:

The Genome Project
22557 NorthWest Pennsylvania Avenue
Washington, D.C. 20225

Dr. Christopher Robertson
8990 Rothchild Way
Las Vegas, NV 89129

Dear Dr. Robertson:

Our Grant Committee is well aware of the groundbreaking work you have been doing in the field of genetic alteration, with emphasis on interspecies genome manipulation. We want to fund your ongoing research.

To this end, we ask that you accept our grant of TWENTY-FIVE MILLION DOLLARS ($25,000,000). Our only conditions for your use of this grant money are these:

1. You will write one or more papers annually for publication in our scientific journal ***The Genome Project Report***, informing the scientific community of your discoveries.
2. You will welcome at least one visit annually from our scientists at your research facility, where you will fill them in on your research.

Please call me at your earliest convenience so that we may discuss your acceptance of this grant.

Yours truly,

Rachael W. Blythe

Rachael Wittington Blythe, Director
(202) 436-9705

"Twenty-five million dollars!" Andy and I screamed out in almost perfect unison.

"Yep," Dad said with a huge grin. "And the funny thing is, I didn't even apply for a grant from The Genome Project. Rachael says they heard about my work when your *SpinoRex* poison responded to the anti-toxin and the news people did some interviews with me. They checked me out and decided they wanted to fund a new laboratory and my research. Simple as that!" He reached out, picked up the letter, folded it with a flourish and tucked it back in his pocket.

And that is how it happened. Over the next six months, the new laboratory building took shape on the mountainside, with floor-to-ceiling windows that would allow Dad and his future staff of scientists to enjoy the city view while they worked; but since the windows were one-way glass, the work in the labs could continue in secret... until Dad wanted something revealed to scientists or the public, of course. I know that the one-way glass was practical for security, but I think it made Dad's lab look like a crown of jewels perched near the mountaintop. It was beautiful!

As we left the house on Opening Day for the new laboratory building, Dad pulled me aside and said, "Son, I have a little surprise for you. Stick close to me when we're doing the building walk-through, ok?"

"OK," I said, with curiosity mounting. "What sort of surprise?"

"You'll see," Dad said. When he said nothing more, I took his cue and remained silent for the 15-minute ride to the new lab. By the time we arrived, there were news crews all over the place. Dad got out of the car and they all zeroed in on him, with holo-mics and cameras at the ready. Dad said a few quick words, then led the crowd to the main entrance, where Security had arranged for "multiple entries" through the building's protection system. I had to dodge people, holo-mics and cameras to try to "stick close" to Dad as everyone pushed and shoved to get the best view of all the shiny new lab equipment, taking holo after photo after more holos.

Dad did a great job as "tour guide" through it all, but I noticed one curious thing: The equipment that Dad always used for his genetics experiments was nowhere to be seen. It occurred to me then that Dad was cleverly showing off his new facility while not letting anyone in on the experiments going on there.

We were nearly at the back of the lab building when Dad reached out for me, turned to the news crews and said, "Folks, this building will actually serve a dual purpose. When I open these doors, I will invite you – and my son Daniel – to see for the first time…" With a flourish, he ripped off the brown paper that had hidden the foot-high golden lettering above the doorway… "TEAM TRIASSIC HEADQUARTERS & TRAINING FACILITY."

He pushed open the huge double doors and I gasped. Before me was an enormous gym surrounded by a complex of offices, small lounges and study rooms; in each corner was a two-story storage area filled to overflowing with both familiar and all-new training equipment for my Team. High on the far wall of the gym was a holo-screen that looked a little familiar.

"What's that, Dad?" I asked, pointing at it.

Before Dad had a chance to answer, Elliott's voice boomed, "IT IS I, DANIEL! DON'T YOU RECOGNIZE ME? I AM CRUSHED!"

OMG! Somehow Dad had arranged to transfer all our Team Triassic stuff – *including Elliott, our ultra-tech computer*, whose wall-screen was now immense – from our city gym to this massive new facility and to pack in piles of new equipment. Unbelievable – that it all happened within hours, after we left training last night! Then I saw the heads of my whole Team peeking out from the doors of the rooms surrounding the gym, and I realized that Dad and my Team had worked this magic to surprise me.

With tears flooding my eyes, I managed to say, "Th-thanks, Dad. I don't know what to say…"

My Team dashed over to surround us in a big group-hug. Dad looked a little teary-eyed himself as he drew me close. "You deserve this and so much more, son," he said, as holo-cameras recorded everything for the ***Evening News.***

Well, they could not record *everything*...

It seems that Dad and – to my complete surprise – MATTHEW had collaborated on many parts of the design of our training facility. Now, I know Matthew was pretty outstanding when it came to designing things in our middle school Robotics class, but I never thought that his design expertise extended to architecture, especially to groundbreaking, never-before-seen construction elements like a Team Triassic training facility!

After the media folks left and Dad, my Team and I were left alone in our new Headquarters, Juli and Kayla made their way to the front of the group.

"We need you all to take a seat in one of those chairs over there," Kayla said, gesturing to a row of folding chairs lined up in front of the office area. As we all shuffled our way toward the chairs, Juli's voice almost exploded from her mouth in excitement:

"We have something to show you that is SO COOL!" She was already dashing across the gym toward the Control Room when she repeated over her shoulder, "It is SO COOL and YOU WILL LOVE IT!" Kayla jogged across the gym to catch up with her and they both disappeared behind the door with **CONTROL No Entry** on a plaque overhead.

In a few seconds, their voices rang through loudspeakers that echoed all around the gym.

Kayla was first. "Everybody ready? LOOK UP!"

A faint whirring sound drew our attention to what we all probably thought was a normal gym ceiling, but it was not what it appeared to be. In less than fifteen seconds, the entire ceiling disappeared into… somewhere … and we were looking at the sky.

Juli had obviously prepared a little narrative to go with all of this. As the ceiling disappeared, she said, "For realism in our training, and with particular sensitivity to the larger dino hybrids among us, this open ceiling is essential. But alone, this is not good enough when it comes to realism for our training. Now look down."

As we drew our attention back to the gym itself, something was happening to the floor. The surface that had appeared to be constructed of 10-by-10 foot sections of rigid, stretched canvas (like that in a boxing ring) was swelling, changing shape and growing taller. Within less than two minutes, we could see that the gym was now filling with realistic-looking sections of buildings that any Las Vegas resident could recognize.

"That's the Stratosphere!" Timeer yelled, pointing at the familiar "feet" that supported the city's iconic tower, now extended through the open roof.

"And Fremont Street!" Lynnelle cried, when the well-known lighted canopy stretched out before us.

As one familiar city site after another emerged from the floor level, we were all stunned. Soon the Rio's curved red and blue glass rose against the far left wall and a 737 took off from McCarran as the Paris Hotel's Eiffel Tower grew before our eyes in the center of everything.

Juli's voice brought us all to attention when she said – almost apologetically – that this "configuration" for training was just the first of five training designs that were planned. "We just didn't get finished with the technical things in time for the Open House," she said. "Sorry, guys!"

One of the girls must have pushed a button then, because the city of Las Vegas seemed to melt slowly into the floor, which took on its original stretched canvas appearance, and the roof slid closed.

As Kayla and Juli emerged from the Control Room, the rest of us sprinted across the gym floor, jumping, whooping and hollering, and grabbed them in a group hug. Looking around, I noticed that Matthew had stayed in his chair near the office area. I turned and called to him, but he stayed where he was and looked down.

I ran over to him. "What's the matter, Matthew? This is a great day and you were a big part of making it happen. You should be proud!"

He didn't look up. In a soft voice, he said, "It's my fault the configurations aren't all ready. It took me too long to program everything. I'm a lot better at design than I am at computer programming. I am afraid your Dad is disappointed in me."

"Disappointed?! Are you kidding? What other kid could have created *any* configuration? NO ONE! Now, come over here and let us congratulate you on the amazing job you have done here." I pulled him out of his chair and walked him to the center of the gym, where the rest of Team Triassic were gathered around my Dad.

"Ah, here he is!" Dad said, coming up to shake Matthew's hand. "I was hoping I'd have the chance to let your Team know that it was you alone who came up with the idea of transforming a plain training floor into replicas of areas where your battles will likely occur. You are one extraordinary young man, Matthew. I can't wait to see what other configurations are still in that head of yours!"

Matthew ducked his head and said, "Th-thank you, sir." Then he broke into a spasm of sobs, gasps and hiccups that drew us all around him. Anyone looking at this scene would have thought we were comforting our friend after a tragedy, when just the opposite had occurred. Our friend was a creative prodigy and we were celebrating his remarkable achievement!

All through the months of construction of his new lab facility, Dad had continued to work in our garage most days, traveling up to Lone Mountain a few times each week. It wasn't until Opening Day that I learned he had insisted at the outset that the construction schedule would complete his new Genetic Alteration Room (GAR) <u>first</u>. This was because of his promise to Nick just three months after my release from Centennial Hills... that he would alter Nick's dino hybrid DNA to duplicate my *Regem Insuprabilus* hybrid. At the time, the new lab building's completion was still months away. But the GAR was a necessity, since there was no way that Nick, at five feet-nine, could fit into the suitcase-sized Genetic Alteration Chamber that Dad had used to alter DNA in Andy and me years ago.

The new GAR was about the size of our home's coat closet. Once a person entered it for alteration through a tempered glass door, he was instructed to back up against the right wall, from which curved, padded restraints then emerged to secure him as the entire GAR rotated ninety degrees, allowing the person to relax... lying down for the entire alteration procedure.

Nick's alteration had happened in mid-February. At the time, I was under the impression that his new dino hybrid would be an exact duplicate of my own; but I was unaware that Nick and Dad had secretly agreed to include a tiny variance from the Proprietary Blend of my "recipe" with Nick's alteration. Dad doubled the Cuttlefish portion and eliminated the

Tree Frog… "Just to be different," he had explained to Nick, who was 100% OK with it. Would this small change make any difference in Nick's *Regem Insuprabilus?* Who knows?

We were all still juggling a modified school schedule with the demands of training at that time, so Nick had been looking forward to skipping classes for a week or so for his genetic alteration and follow-up monitoring. I remember that he was almost as excited about having a school-free week as he was about the alteration itself. Unfortunately for Nick's hopes and dreams, Dad's secretary scheduled his alteration for February 10th, the Friday before Presidents Day, after which Clark County Schools had scheduled three days of in-service training for teachers and staff. This led into a county-wide rally on that Friday, promoting the district's four-year goal of "0% HIGH SCHOOL DROPOUTS!" So there would be *no school* the whole time Nick was out.

I was with Nick when he compared his alteration schedule with the school calendar.

"They have GOT to be kidding!" he wailed. He waited a few seconds, then asked, "Do you think your Dad would reschedule me?"

I just looked at him. My Dad had agreed to donate his time and his expertise FOR FREE, just to make Nick – and me, to some degree – happy, and to strengthen Team Triassic. There was no way that I would be any part of asking him to change anything.

The look on my face must have been enough to make Nick reconsider, because he looked down and said, very softly, "Uh, I guess not. I don't want to sound like I don't appreciate it."

He paused, then looked up, took a deep breath and said, "The most important thing is that this little *Velociraptor* will soon be a second *Regem Insuprabilus.* The sooner that happens, the better!"

Chapter 5

With Nick's alteration taken care of, Matthew was next. Near the end of April, Dad's busy research schedule again loosened up a bit, so he was able to fit Matthew's alteration into the calendar. Since I just happened to be passing by Dad's office on April 20th when Matthew came in for his pre-procedure interview, he waved me over.

"Hey, Daniel, could you sit in on this meeting with your Dad? My parents have given their permission for the genetic alteration, but I have a few special requests. I could use your support."

"Sure," I said, "but the decisions are really yours and Dad's. What input do you need from me?"

"Well, you know what the Team needs from each of us," he said. "Besides, there's something I know I *don't* want, and you will be able to help me explain why to your Dad."

I had no idea what he was referring to, but I just said, "OK, let's go," and we knocked on the frame of Dad's open door.

"Come in, guys," Dad called, "and have a seat."

Over the next ten minutes, Dad explained how the GAR works, what residual effects Matthew might expect and the necessity for his patience as his body would be adjusting to its new genomes. It was an almost "canned" description that Dad would provide for everyone before their date with the GAR. When he finished, he paused and asked, "So Matthew, do you have any questions for me about the procedure?"

Matthew glanced at me, swallowed hard, and said, "Well-ll... I know you have a recipe prepared for my new hybrid, but..." He stopped, obviously unsure of how to go on.

"But what?" Dad prompted, kindly.

"Well-ll," he started again, and stopped again. He looked at me for help, but I had no idea what I was supposed to say.

"Matthew, spit it out!" I said, maybe a little harshly. "Tell Dad what you want him to know."

"OK," he said, looking down. Then he almost whispered, "I don't want to *look* like a *Spinosaurus*," he said, still examining his feet.

"But that's your primary genome," Dad said. "The one you were born with."

"That's the problem," Matthew said. "Everybody still associates me with the *Spino-Rex* that attacked Molasky, because I look a lot like that beast when I morph in training. The girls look at me funny – and Kayla even once asked if I was *related* to that *Spino-Rex* – so I am hoping my alteration can get rid of the *Spinosaurus* genome completely... or at least get rid of what shows on the outside."

Dad leaned back in his chair, rubbed his chin and thought for a moment. Matthew looked at me, probably for encouragement, but I just stared ahead, waiting for Dad to say something. At least three minutes went by before Dad pulled his chair up to his desk, folded his hands on top of the folder with MATTHEW WILLIAMS on the tab and smiled.

"Matthew, your request has offered me a challenge: Until now, I have never tried to *extract* an inborn hybrid genome from a research subject. My research has focused on *adding* the DNA of other species to the hybrid genome a person was born with. But I think that what you request is possible, and I accept the challenge."

Matthew cried in pure joy, jumping up to lean over Dad's desk and grab his hand. "Thank you, thank you, THANK YOU!"

"So let me do some figuring," Dad said. A few minutes went by while he scribbled notes on a notepad. Then he said, "I'll have a plan ready in a few days." He winked at me, and then looked at Matthew.

"Now, let me make sure I have the details correct... You don't mind if the *external* appearance of your *Spinosaurus* remains intact; you just don't want any of the *Spinosaurus* innards, right?"

"NO! NO!" Matthew yelled, jumping up, horrified. Then he saw our faces and realized that Dad was joking.

"Oh, you guys!" he said, and we all cracked up.

Before the April meeting between Matthew and Dad, I had figured that the GAR would turn Matthew into a SpinoRaptor: Once morphed, he would still look like a *Spinosaurus*, but his *Velociraptor* traits would be enhanced. When Dad learned how important it was to Matthew that he would no longer look mostly like a *Spinosaurus* when he morphed, however, Dad came up with a new protocol to minimize Matthew's visible *Spinosaurus* features while maintaining the powerful internal qualities of this inborn dino hybrid.

Because the GAR procedure for Matthew would be including the extraction of some of his inborn *Spinosaurus* genome, we were all told not to expect to see our friend for training for "at least three weeks post-GAR."

Near the end of May, we all arrived on a Monday at the Lone Mountain facility at the usual time for training. To our surprise, Nick was already in the break room with his brother Angel – who was not generally the most prompt member of our Team – and they both had "We know something that you don't know" smirks on their faces.

"What's up?" I asked, as the rest of the Team joined me.

As usual, both Kayla and Lynnelle had their hands on their hips. Lynnelle took a step forward and said, "Yeah, Nick, what's up? Is this another one of your pranks?"

The rest of us looked at each other, confused.

"Pranks?" Juli asked. "What pranks?"

Nick stood up quickly, saying, "They're nothing… nothing important. Just silliness between Lynnelle and me." He cleared his throat, swallowed, then went on. "Let's go into the gym and we'll show you something you may just want to see…" He led us toward the rear gym doors.

With a flourish and a "TA-DA!" Nick flipped on the lights. Standing across the gym from us was a dinosaur in full extension. It was different from any dino any of us had ever seen: twelve feet tall, the basic shape and claws of an oversized *Velociraptor*, a few plates on its back up near the neck, a sail running down the spine and a powerful, flat tail that looked deadly. Completely different from all of us, yet the way it was "posed" looked somehow familiar…

I heard a couple of the members of the Team take the deep breath they needed to morph for a fight with this unknown dino, but Nick put up his hand.

"No morphing, guys," he said. "He's a friend, a brand-new *Velociospinus*."

As he said that, the formidable beast across from us roared once, then de-morphed. Within a minute, before us stood Matthew!

"OMG!" we all shouted, as we ran across the gym to gather our friend in a group-hug. Everyone spoke at once: "Matthew, we missed you!" "Welcome back, Bro!" "Gosh, I'd never recognize you!" "What happened to your *Spinosaurus*?" "Do you feel all right?" "Are you back 100%?"

Matthew grinned as he tried to answer everybody's questions, but mostly he just seemed to be enjoying the hug.

"I missed you guys," he said. "Glad to be back." He hesitated a moment, then looked around the group as he spoke. "While I was in recovery, I worked on the training configurations. They are coming along, but it'll still take me a little time to get everything right. I hope you can be patient with me."

Nick patted him on his back. "You'll have all the time you need. Great to have you back, Bro!"

Dear Diary,

Today was a special day at Headquarters, because Matthew came back to us. We have missed him so much! But he scared us all half to death because he showed up in his new Velociospinus hybrid form. When Nick and the guys called us all into the gym, and Nick had a smirk on his face, I knew he had something up his sleeve. Lately, he has been pulling pranks on me (I don't know why) and I haven't noticed him pranking any of the guys or even Kayla or Juli...but maybe it's just Nick's way of loosening the tension we all feel. I have to wonder, though... Why are the pranks only on me? Even Juli has started to notice this. Yesterday she asked if I thought that Nick's pranks are his weird way of saying he likes me. Like really LIKES me. I told her I didn't think so, but now I am not so sure. He IS really cute, so I don't think it would be a bad thing at all if his pranks meant something.

I would feel a lot better if Nick's pranks weren't so public, though. Last Tuesday I was running late after completing a map update, so I was happy to see that he had saved me a seat at our recap meeting. Just as I was about to sit, he nudged my leg out from under me a little so I plopped down hard, setting off THREE Whoopie Cushions he had tucked under the chair cover. It was the loudest fart sound I ever heard! I was so embarrassed. Nick just laughed and laughed... He could hardly control himself. The other guys laughed, too, except for Daniel, who was trying to get the meeting started.

Could a thing like this mean he's looking for a relationship? If so, I would really like him to find another way to show me! When I think about it, though, I do kind of wish my prankster was Daniel.

Lynnelle

Over the summer, Timeer's procedure in Dad's GAR enhanced his original *Suchomimus* genome with *Pteranodon* DNA. He emerged from the GAR a *Volanto Crocotalus* (Flying Clawed Reptile) which gave Team Triassic a *second* flying dino hybrid. Timeer and Andy spent nearly all of August practicing high-speed ascents, dives and swoops over and around Mount Charleston, far outside of the city's "no-fly" zones. Andy's *Avian Sinustrodon*'s orange and gold body and copper bat-like wings glistened in the sun as his condor-sized body flew in circles around Timeer's *Volanto Crocotalus*, his much-larger flying partner, whose green, blue and purple feathers looked iridescent with every movement. The ruffled feathers, ripped hides and broken claws they experienced early on became less and less as their reaction timing and airborne braking ability improved.

By early September, Andy announced to the Team, "Team Triassic's Flying Division is READY!"

This meant that Team Triassic was now prepared for anything that would come our way. I said as much to Dad as we headed to the car for the short drive to Lone Mountain one September morning. Even though I generally walked to training, Dad had said he wanted to drive me that day, so it was obvious he had something on his mind.

As he settled in and started the car, he glanced over at me, then looked straight ahead as he said, "So kiddo, I've been working on some armor that morphs with you as your Team members turn into your dinos," he said, matter-of-factly.

I lost my concentration for a few seconds, trying to process what he was saying. "Armor that morphs?" I sat up straight in my seat.

Unaware of my startled reaction, Dad continued: "The suits are designed to morph with your dinos, hopefully protecting you kids from any dangerous dinos out there."

I didn't really want to question Dad, but I felt it important to mention one thing: "Some of us already have some sort of armor on our bodies when we morph, Dad."

"But not all of you," Dad reminded me, "and not everywhere on your bodies. I first started working on this when Andy kept coming home from Mount Charleston with gashes, broken fingers and clumps ripped out of his hair. The armor I am designing will be individually fitted to your Team Members *wherever* any of you will need its protection. OK?"

"OK!" I cried. "It's awesome… Thanks, Dad!" He had remedied a problem for Team Triassic that none of us had realized even existed… and which would probably save us from wounds – or worse – in battle. Dad's genius never ceases to amaze me!

As the car climbed the switchback road up to the lab, I rested my head back on the seat, closed my eyes, and let my mind wander. Almost like a movie trailer, scenes from the last year came into focus, then faded as the next scene emerged, followed by another and another. I saw our fabulous new Training Headquarters on that Opening Day, each new Team Member hybrid as he emerged from his post-GAR, some "bloopers" from of our recent training exercises, Andy and Timeer announcing our Flying Division "READY," and now Dad telling me about protective armor for everyone!

Last November as my friends and I left Molasky Stadium on the day we were introduced to the world as Team Triassic, I said we were "magnificent." I wonder what word describes something that is BETTER than "magnificent," because that word – whatever it is – definitely describes us now.

I am SO proud of us!

"See you tonight, Dan!" Dad's voice brought me back from my daydream, as he got out of the car, grabbed some folders out of the backseat and headed to the lab.

"See you, Dad," I called. "And THANKS!"

Chapter 9

Even though it seemed that Nick and I were seeing less and less of each other, as we had different duties with Team Triassic's training, we did sit together in the Headquarters break room each Friday in front of a desk-size "Elliott" to plan the training schedule for the next week. Most of our training exercises took place inside the large gym, with or without one of two floor configurations Matthew had completed by summer's end. In addition to the City of Las Vegas configuration, we now had a Desert and Mountains setting that gave us a whole new perspective on battling out where Nature could sometimes be as much of an adversary as a hybrid dino.

I found this out the hard way one afternoon when I backed into a saguaro cactus while sparring at 25% extension with Timeer's *Volanto Crocotalus*. I spent the next ninety minutes pulling cactus needles out of the only part of my legs not protected naturally with armor. (So Dad was right… We ALL need his prosthetic armor!) I did ask Kayla and Juli afterwards if we *really* needed all that "realism" in our training, hoping that the cactus would end up in the warehouse. But the saguaro remained part of the Desert and Mountains configuration and I just made sure to don Dad's leg armor before future sparring there.

So every Friday, we made a schedule that ensured each fighting Team member would spar at least once during the week with the other dino hybrids on the Team. The only exception was Kayla, who had been pulling double duty as part of the fighting Team and as Juli's partner in Control;

generally, Kayla did only light sparring in the City configuration and martial arts workouts on the canvas. I was happy that she wanted to keep up with her battling skills, because you just never know if or when we might need an extra pair of claws!

When posted on "Big Elliott," a typical weekly schedule would look like this:

Day/Time	Configuration	Aggressor	Defender	Result
Monday/10 am	City	Matthew	Andy*	
Monday/2 pm	City	Timeer	Lynnelle	
Tuesday/10am	Desert/Mountains	Angel*	Michael	
Tuesday/2pm	Desert/Mountains	Daniel	Nick	
Wednesday/10 am	Canvas	Nick	Johnny	
Wednesday/2 pm	Canvas	Kayla	Juli	
Thursday/10 am	City	Michael	Daniel	
Thursday/2pm	City	Johnny	Kayla	
Friday/10 am	Desert/Mountains	Lynnelle	Matthew	
Friday/4pm*	Desert/Mountains	Andy*	Angel*	

Times for the starred bouts on the schedule could vary, as the work schedules for Andy and Angel sometimes changed; occasionally, their bouts were pushed over onto Saturday.

The Results column was based on a point system Nick and I came up with – similar to points scored in a boxing match. While dino hybrids were expected to avoid hurting each other, the two opponents earned points by positioning a "death blow" or succeeding with a strategic attack or avoidance move. Each sparring match was divided into three 5-minute rounds, with two-minute rest periods in-between.

Team members took turns as Overseers – the ones watching the match and awarding points. Every match was holo-recorded so we could use these simulated battles in our sit-down training sessions on Tuesdays and Thursdays over lunch.

Our training was also specific to each dino hybrid's special abilities or talents. For example, it was important to train both Andy and Matthew to enhance their innate ability to "sniff out" an adversary. We started by having Lynnelle hide a piece of three-day-old salmon under a big rock on a ledge on the other side of Lone Mountain. After she let Andy's *Avian Sinustrodon* and Matthew's *Velociospirus* sniff the paper the salmon had been wrapped in, they were off – Andy in flight and Matthew galloping along underneath him. I expected that they'd be gone for an hour or so; but less than 13 minutes later, Matthew slid to a halt in front of Lynnelle and me. Andy climbed down off his back, knelt down like a knight presenting the spoils of war to a monarch. Just as he was about to hand me the salmon, Matthew's *Velociospirus* head whipped around, grabbed the fish and swallowed it in one gulp.

"Eewww!" cried Lynnelle, grossed out completely.

As Matthew de-morphed, he was still licking his lips. "Sashimi!" he said with a grin.

We made better choices to challenge our two "sniffers" after that, but no matter how mild a scent their prey gave off or how far away we dragged it, these two guys returned from their trials in record time. It was frustrating but also encouraging… Obviously, we had two super dino hybrid bloodhounds ready to find any hiding adversary.

Chapter 10

Ever since our new Headquarters was completed, our arrangement with the Clark County School District had permitted us to complete our high school coursework on-line. We had several small classrooms available, each one equipped with two computers and large monitors, as well as bookcases for other materials. Each of us had our own section of the bookcases, so we could keep our things organized.

While our new "modern" educational system was efficient and fit nicely around our Team Triassic training schedule, it couldn't include every course we had had in public school. The one course I missed the most was Drama, of course. I had waited for my first Drama class for a long time – especially after I didn't get it the first year I signed up – but there was no way Drama courses could be part of my online schooling at Headquarters. So I just gave up on any hope of pursuing a career on the stage.

I assumed that Kayla and Juli had had to make the same decision – to give up Drama in favor of Team Triassic – so imagine my surprise when the two of them burst into my office one morning to invite me to their play!

Kayla gushed, "Daniel, we want you to be the first to know that Juli and I *both* got parts in the Spring Mountain Little Theater's next production of 'Annie Get Your Gun!'"

I sat up straight, shocked, and tried to look happy for them. When I didn't actually *say* anything, they went on, excitedly.

"Kayla is Annie Oakley, Daniel… Can you believe it? The LEAD!" Juli almost screamed.

"And Juli is my sister Nellie," Kayla said. "We get to sing 'Doin' What Comes Natur'lly' together!"

Now, this occasion obviously called for some heartfelt (appearing) congratulations, but – to be honest – my dominant feeling at that moment was…JEALOUSY! I had to call upon my best acting skills to appear to be absolutely, totally thrilled for them both. (And I really *wanted* to be thrilled… It was just hard right at that moment.)

"Wow, that's FABULOUS!" I enthused. "I didn't even know you were trying out."

"We decided not to say anything to anybody until we found out if we made it," Juli said. "No reason to get people riled up about scheduling…"

Scheduling! That's going to be a problem, I thought. I remembered all those many hours play rehearsals consumed. *How will rehearsals leave time for their Team duties and online classes?*

Kayla was way ahead of me. She pointed her holo at the wall screen and a weekly calendar appeared.

"Juli's Team shifts are shown in green and mine are in orange," she said. "You will see that we will still be available the same number of hours as before. Our rehearsals are Tuesday, Thursday and Saturday, 5 pm to 9 pm – shown in blue."

I was about to ask a question, but Juli put up her pointer finger, telling me to hold off.

"I know you are concerned about Team emergencies, Daniel." I nodded and she went on. "We have the word of Hector Bigelow, our director, that we can always have our holos with us and on, and that we can leave rehearsal on a moment's notice if you need us."

There was nothing more for me to say. The girls had it all figured out. So I stood up and gathered them both in a hug.

"So when are the performances?" I asked. "I want to get a ticket before they're sold out!" *This was no time for jealousy,* I told myself. *Kayla and Juli are so excited and all I should be feeling right now is happiness for them.* What I said next was not acting – I was completely sincere:

"I can't wait to see you on stage," I said, and I meant it. "Congratulations!"

Chapter II

A few days later, we were in the middle of one of our Tuesday sit-down sessions when Elliott's voice interrupted things with a polite "HMMM… EXCUSE ME, DANIEL?"

I turned toward Elliott's screen and saw the image of a kid standing outside the gate to the lab complex. He walked back and forth, obviously trying to figure a way inside, but our security was top-notch.

As we watched the kid, Elliott explained, "DANIEL, THIS YOUNG MAN HAS BEEN OUTSIDE THE GATE FOR NEARLY AN HOUR. I FINALLY ASKED HIM WHAT HIS BUSINESS IS AND HE JUST ASKED TO SPEAK TO YOU. I SCANNED HIM AND I BELIEVE HIM TO BE NO THREAT. ARE YOU AVAILABLE TO SEE THIS YOUNG MAN?"

We had just about finished reviewing last week's training anyway, so I asked Juli if she would go get the kid and bring him to my office.

"You got it," she said and she was off. I headed to the office while Nick and the other Team members dispersed to take care of their individual responsibilities. About three minutes later, Juli stood at our office doorway with the kid. He was a little smaller than Juli, had short, dirty blond hair that looked like it hadn't been combed recently and he wore thick glasses. I could tell right away he was very nervous.

"Come in and have a seat," I said, standing up and putting on my most welcoming smile. The kid jumped back, startled. Then he got his act together and sat down.

Juli pulled the door closed with a "click" and the kid jumped in his seat.

"Hey, you ok?" I asked.

He ducked his head and looked up only using his eyes, staring at me with an anxious look.

"I-I'm- I'm fine," he said, looking down at his lap.

I walked up to him and held my hand out. "I'm Daniel. And you are...?."

He looked up and slowly reached out but hesitated before grabbing my hand in a very sweaty handshake.

"I'm... My name is Xander — with an X, not a Z," he said softly, crossing his arms in an X.

I sat down and turned to face him. "Well, it's nice to meet you, Xander. Are you sure you are ok? You seem pretty nervous."

His head finally came up, and he said, with sudden conviction, "No... I'm NOT ok. And I think you and your Team are the only people who can help me."

"What's wrong?" I asked, looking intently into his eyes.

As he began his story, he turned away and started to shake. He had obviously suffered some real trauma.

He stared out the window as he began, with a quiver in his voice, "When I was eleven years old, my Mom and I were attacked by a gang of *Velociraptors*."

I sat up in my seat and leaned forward, eager to hear more. "Can you tell me about it?" I asked.

He turned his head, locked eyes with me and took a deep breath, then closed his eyes. As he talked, I could tell he was reliving a terrible incident.

"My Mom and I went to the store. When we walked out to get to the car, three *Velociraptors* cornered us. She screamed and told me to run. Two of them pounced on my Mom and the other bit my arm." He rolled up his sleeve to reveal a large, ugly scar. "I was able to get away with only this, but my Mom..." Tears filled his eyes.

He stood up and walked to the back of the room. "An ambulance came and took her to the hospital. She never came home. Doctors could easily fix her physical injuries, but ever since that day she has been in what the doctors call a 'waking coma state.'"

"A *waking coma?*" I cried. "How is that different from a regular coma?"

"Mom's brain function is just like a comatose patient's brain, the doctors explained, but her eyes are open when her body isn't sleeping. Most days, the nurses strap her carefully into a wheelchair and position her next to the window with a great view of the valley. I don't think she really sees anything, though. When I go to visit her, she just stares into space. I don't think she knows me." Tears snaked their way down both cheeks.

I stood up and walked over to him, putting my hand on his shoulder.

"Xander, people recover from comas all the time. I myself am a perfect example… Last year I was in a coma for over a month, but I have recovered completely."

He shook his head sadly. "It's been nearly five *years* for Mom, though," he said, using his sleeve to wipe the tears off his cheeks. "It's different."

"You can't give up hope, though," I told him. "Medical breakthroughs and miracles happen all the time. Just try to be optimistic… even though I know it is tough."

He turned around and wrapped his arms around me. We were both quiet for a couple of minutes.

Then he pushed back, took a halting breath, shook his head a little and asked, "Uh, is there a restroom I could use?" I could tell he was clearly embarrassed by tears that showed no sign of stopping.

"Sure," I said. "Turn left out the door and it's the third door."

When he opened the office door, Nick was standing there, his arm raised, ready to knock. Xander jumped a little, then scooted through the door and turned toward the restroom.

Nick came in with a "What's up?" look on his face. I filled him in on Xander's sad story. When the kid returned, he had washed his face and composed himself, so I just introduced him to Nick quickly and we all sat down.

Nick turned in his chair to look directly at Xander. He said, "I know a little how you feel. When Daniel was in his coma, I was scared for him. I thought he was going to die. But look at him today! Always have hope for your Mom."

"I try to… but it's been so long. It's hard," he said, and he looked like more tears were on the way. Then he took a deep breath and said, "But this isn't why I came here."

Both Nick and I stayed silent, as Xander found the words he wanted.

"Ever since the *Velociraptor* attack, I think I've been scarred for life, and not just on my arm. I'm scared all the time that it will happen again," he said, in a quivering voice. "I was hoping Team Triassic could teach me how not to be afraid." He stopped, then asked, "Do you take apprentice Team members?"

Nick and I looked at each other and smiled.

"Well, we don't have an apprentice program as such," Nick said, "but I think we may be able to find a spot for you." He pulled our office-sized Elliott over to Xander so he could give our system some basic information. We listened as Xander told Elliott the details:

"My name is Xander – that's with an X, not a Z – last name Montgomery. On my last birthday, I turned fifteen. I live with my Dad, but my grandparents live in Northwest Las Vegas, so I am there a lot, too." He looked away from the screen and said to me, "You might know our street. It's right near Centennial High School."

Then Elliott showed his usual impatience with any delays (except his own, of course.) In a testy voice, the screen said, "I'm WAITING… SO I BELIEVE YOU ARE NOT A DINO HYBRID. IS THIS CORRECT, XANDER-WITH-AN-X?"

"Right. I'm not a dino hybrid of any sort," Xander replied, probably wondering how Elliott knew this. "That's part of the problem. If I was a dino, I wouldn't've been so scared. I would've fought," he said, "and maybe my Mom would be ok."

"Well, dino or not, you are welcome here," I said, walking over to throw my arm around his shoulder as we all headed for the door. "Some of our training is in martial arts, which is great for self-defense, so it is just right for you, I think. And I KNOW that Juli will be happy to have you here. She's not a dino hybrid, either."

Just about everybody in Las Vegas knows that the primary reason we formed Team Triassic was to prepare for another assault by one or more rogue dino hybrids like last year's *SpinoRex*. We all knew that it was only a matter of time before whoever created the beast I fought at Molasky would threaten our city with more dino hybrid mayhem. This meant that our training protocol focused on battle tactics we would need to know to repel these oversized beasts.

This narrow focus for our training changed when Xander joined us. Two incidents in his second week with us showed just how traumatized he was. The worst one took place the day we decided that one way to make Xander feel a part of our Team was to let him participate in one of our realistic training exercises. Since he had no dino DNA, we thought it might be a challenge for Andy's and Matthew's "super-sniffer" dino hybrids to locate Xander if he hid in a place where other humans were around. It was a slow Friday for us and Andy's work shift had been cancelled, so it seemed like a good idea – at the time.

Privately that afternoon, I had asked Lynnelle to take Xander over to the Red Rock picnic area where he could find a good hiding place.

Before they left, I pulled Xander aside. "Are you ok with this, Xander?" I asked. "I know you are scared of dinos – with good reason – but these are Team Triassic dino hybrids and this is only a training exercise. They won't hurt you."

He said, "Sure, OK, I guess," but he didn't sound convinced.

"Let's consider this part of *your* Team Triassic training then, ok?"

That seemed to make a difference to Xander. He brightened a little and said, "Whatever it takes for me to be part of the Team. Let's do it!"

After Lynnelle and Xander had left for Red Rock, I called Andy and Matthew on my holo. "Meet me outside the gate in five minutes," I told them. "I have a new training challenge for you."

Matthew arrived first. When Andy joined us, I said, "OK, guys, today I want you to find Xander."

"What – Is he missing?" Andy asked, sounding concerned.

I laughed. "No… He is your training challenge for today. I want you to sniff him out. He's away from Lone Mountain. That's all I will tell you. Except for this: Remember that Xander has been traumatized by dinos, so DO NOT TOUCH HIM when you locate him. De-morph when you are at least five feet from him. Then call Lynnelle to come pick the three of you up. Got it?

"Got it!" Matthew said and Andy nodded.

Without another word, Andy morphed into his *Avian Sinustrodon* and Matthew into his *Velociospirus*. The two quickly sniffed Xander's jacket, then they were off.

Not even twenty minutes later, I saw Andy's *Avian Sinustrodon* in the air coming back to Lone Mountain. Matthew's *Velociospinus* followed closely on the ground. As they approached where I was standing, I saw to my horror that Andy was holding a very limp Xander in one of his claws. My brother swooped to a landing, de-morphing as soon as his feet touched the ground. He was just placing Xander on the ground as Matthew arrived and de-morphed.

A completely terrified, sobbing Xander curled into a fetal position up against a cypress tree trunk, covering his head as though he expected another assault.

I couldn't believe my eyes. I ran over and knelt down next to Xander, reached out my hand to touch his back to comfort him, but then thought better of it. Without touching him, I spoke softly, "Xander, talk to us. Are you ok?"

Xander said nothing as he continued to sob and shake from fear.

I stood up and marched over to Andy and Matthew, furious. "WHAT THE HELL! I TOLD YOU TO NOT TOUCH HIM!" I screamed.

"I- I forgot. I just got excited when I saw him…" Andy said, looking down.

"THAT DOESN'T MATTER, ANDY! I TOLD YOU STRAIGHT UP TO NOT TOUCH HIM! He's still overcoming a long-standing trauma. WHAT WERE YOU *THINKING?*"

When I turned to Matthew, he shrugged. "I got there late," he said simply.

I was beyond furious then and I didn't really trust myself to act rationally, so I just said, in a quiet but firm voice, "Andy… go home."

"What — why?" Andy asked.

"Just grab your stuff and go home," I said.

Andy shook his head with a sad look on his face. For a minute, I thought my big brother was going to cry. Then he went over and knelt in front of Xander, making a point of *not* touching him, and said with real compassion, "I'm sorry, man."

Xander still said nothing as he continued to shake.

I put my hand on Andy's shoulder. "It's time for you to go," I said. Andy stood up and walked through the door to Headquarters. He looked like a beaten adversary and I felt sorry for him. After all, he's my brother. But he really messed up that day. My biggest fear was that this incident would set Xander back too much. He had been so eager to be part of Team Triassic and – until that day – he had been making great progress in learning self-defense and martial arts.

Although I hadn't told Matthew to leave, he followed Andy into Headquarters, putting his arm around Andy's shoulders and leaning close to talk to him. I hoped he was saying things that would help my brother recover from making such a horrible mistake, telling him our Team is strong and we could – and would — deal with it. These are things I simply could not say to my brother at that time.

By the time I got home, I had cooled off quite a bit about Andy's screw-up with the afternoon's outdoor scent-training drill. While it was still on my mind, my fury had changed mostly to disappointment; I still couldn't understand WHY Andy failed to follow my very clear instructions NOT to touch Xander.

I knocked lightly on his bedroom door, then poked my head in. He was on his bed, facing the far wall. He looked at me over his shoulder, but he didn't say anything. Under lowered brows, he seemed to be trying to figure out why I was there… to continue my afternoon tirade maybe?

"Uh, Bro… Can I come in? We need to talk," I said in my kindest tone.

Turning toward me on his bed, he said, "Sure, come in and have a seat."

Well, in Andy's room that was easier said than done. Neither of us would win any award for neatness, but Andy's room contained a huge virtual reality simulator, some musical instruments scattered about, two flat screen TVs on a long dresser, a chair piled high with sports paraphernalia, and piles of clothes and other things everywhere. After looking around, I shoved some clothes from one corner of his bed and sat down, turning to face him as best I could.

"Look, Bro," I began, "I'm sorry if I went off on you so bad today. I just couldn't believe that you completely ignored what I told you!"

Andy hesitated, looked down and said, "Well, to be honest, I wasn't really listening to you. I had just taken out my earbuds and I was still hearing 'Gotta Rock You NOW!' in my head. Then, before I knew it, Matthew and I were heading to Red Rock and a few minutes later I spotted Xander hiding behind a rock..."

"Matthew wasn't listening to me, either? I asked. "Didn't he say anything?"

"He got there about three seconds after I had grabbed Xander. He roared something — maybe 'Don't touch him' – but it was too late. Xander drooped – I think he fainted – so I decided we should just get him back to Headquarters as fast as possible. I picked him up and flew to Lone Mountain. You know the rest." He looked down, shaking his head. "I am SO sorry all this happened," he said.

"I'm sorry, too, Bro," I said. "Look, we have the weekend off – and I think we all need it – so let's just plan to get you and Xander – and probably Matthew, too – together with Nick and me first thing Monday. You can apologize to Xander – maybe tell him what you told me, so he knows that what happened was kind of an accident — and we'll see if he still wants to be part of the Team. If he does, we'll work things out, OK?"

"OK… and thanks, Bro." He pulled himself into a sitting position and gave me a hug that felt really good.

Dear Diary,

Today could have been the end of Team Triassic, or at least the end of the Team as we know it. The new kid Xander is really traumatized from what happened to him a few years ago when he and his mother were attacked by a Velociraptor gang. His Mom is STILL hospitalized, suffering from severe mental illness, and Xander is afraid to be touched, especially by any of us in our dino hybrid forms. The kid has been coming along really great, learning martial arts and self-defense, so the guys thought he was ready to be the live "bait" to test the scenting abilities of Andy and Matthew away from our mountain.

Daniel asked me to escort Xander over to a hiding place near Red Rock. I clearly heard Daniel tell both Andy and Matthew NOT to touch Xander... just to point at him or something when they found him, demorph right away and then bring him back.

But Andy ignored what his own brother told him – and Andy KNOWS about Xander's fears – and the next thing we saw was Andy flying up to the mountain with Xander's drooping body in his one claw. I thought he was dead! Andy laid him down on the ground as if nothing was wrong at all, and then all hell broke loose. Even though it turned out that Xander was not hurt at all – physically, that is – Daniel was FURIOUS at his brother. Andy tried to make excuses and

Matthew tried to smooth things over, but Daniel wouldn't listen. He sent his brother home.

I think today we lost at least one original member of Team Triassic, and probably a new one, too. I wonder if we'll ever see either Andy or Xander on Lone Mountain again.

Lynnelle

Even though Xander had holo-texted me on Saturday that he wanted to quit the Team, he agreed to meet with me alone on Monday morning at 8:30. We had a good heart-to-heart talk, but – even so — I wasn't 100% sure he'd changed his mind about quitting by the time the Team arrived at 9. I had already told him what Andy explained to me on Friday in his bedroom, so maybe that's why Xander jumped only a little when Andy and Matthew came through the door. The kid took a deep breath, let it out slowly, and then seemed a lot calmer. He looked at Andy.

"Hi," he said, simply.

"Hi, Xander," Andy replied, carefully keeping his distance from the kid. "Look, man, I'm really sorry about what happened on Friday. It's my fault that I wasn't listening when Daniel told me you still don't like to be touched by any of us. You know, I've watched you in martial arts training a couple of times and you seem to have developed some good moves. Maybe seeing you doing so great in training made me forget that you're still getting over the *Velociraptor* attack. For a non-dino, you are really something, kid!"

Xander's face brightened. "Thanks, Andy," he said.

Matthew chimed in then. "It was partly my fault, Xander. As soon as I saw Andy grab for you, I should have used *Velociraptor* dialect to tell him to stop. Instead, I just roared as a *Velociospirus.* So we are both at fault. For my part, I promise you here and now that you will not EVER have to worry about being touched by me… not until you are ready. And then only if you *tell* us you are ready."

"Same here," Andy said.

Then Xander shocked us all by hesitating only a second then looking up and nodding.

"I'm ready," he said.

"What??" I blurted out. "What do you mean, Xander?"

"Well, my Mom always told me 'There's no time like the present.' If Andy and Matthew would be willing to let me touch THEM in a partial-morphed state, maybe I will be able to stand their touch. Could we try it?"

We all looked at each other, not knowing what to say. Andy broke the silence.

"Fine with me. Let's do it at 25%." Before anyone could stop him, he morphed into a small *Avian Sinustrodon* and extended one of his winged claws toward Xander, who reached out tentatively with his left hand and touched a few of Andy's feathers. He hesitated, then touched the back of Andy's clawed hand and ran his fingers up to the bend in his wing. He looked over his shoulder at me and I nodded a "Go ahead."

Then Xander did what I expect was one of the hardest things of all… he held out his right hand toward Andy's right claw and let Andy touch HIM. This was a scene I never expected to see, especially after Friday's experience.

While Xander was focusing on Andy, Matthew was quietly morphing to his 25%, which is considerably larger than Andy. I was afraid he would scare Xander, but the kid turned around, took in the large *Velociospirus* before him and extended his hand. He jumped back when Matthew moved a little fast toward him, but then we were watching a "handshake" between little Xander and Matthew's 25% *Velociospirus*.

I was so happy I could have burst into tears right then. But no one on Team Triassic needed to see a blubbering Team leader!

Despite the great progress Xander made on that Monday with Andy and Matthew, he was still afraid to walk home from Lone Mountain alone – even after a few weeks of self-defense training. So one of us usually walked along to his house with him. That Wednesday it was my first turn for the walk-along, and I was happy to have the time to get better acquainted with our newest Team member.

As we started down the mountain path, I said, "So you live near Centennial High, right?"

"Yes," he replied. "My brother and I are sophomores."

Since our Team's modified school schedule was still managed through Molasky, I didn't know much about Centennial – except for the little that Andy mentioned from time to time (but that was mostly about how cool it had been to be a sports star because teachers let him get away with everything).

"How are you liking it?" I asked.

"Well, it's all right, I guess," he said, not sounding very convinced. "It's still school. What I can't stand is how all the dino hybrids like to show off their dino traits when my brother and I have none of them," he said, with a little anger in his voice.

I nodded my head. "I guess everything is different in high school," I said. "In middle school, no one dared to show off their dino form. Even if morphing was accidental, you got thrown out of school."

Xander shook his head sadly. "At Centennial, if you're a dino hybrid, you're one of the 'Cool Kids.' Everyone who can't morph is just a nobody," he said.

I wondered to myself just WHY this would be the school culture. What ever happened to the zero tolerance for bullying that we all grew up with? And why was dino morphing allowed at Centennial when it could get you expelled from Molasky?

But as this was not the time for a philosophical discussion, I just said, "It must very hard for you and your brother."

"Yeah, it all changed after the Molasky attack. I think the principal and the teachers decided it would be a put-off to future attacks if the people creating the beasts knew there would be an unknown number of dino hybrids to greet them at the high school. On one level, it makes some sense. But it has really divided the kids into Dino and Not-Dino groups and there is NO crossover!"

I wondered if this division would exist if I hadn't fought off that beast at Molasky. Of course, if I hadn't done that, there may have been some current members of Centennial's freshman class that wouldn't have made it out of middle school...

"Aw, those Centennial dino hybrids are just wannabes," I said with a grin. "Maybe they want to be like Team Triassic, but they're nowhere near as exceptional as we are. And now YOU are one of us. So THERE, Centennial dino-wannabes!" I said, winking at him and sprinting ahead.

He was huffing and puffing when he caught up to me, but he had enough breath to say, "Daniel, I'm so happy that you and Nick took me into the Team right away. I haven't been this happy for … well, for years."

I knew the years he was referring to, of course.

Our route to Xander's house took us past Centennial High. As we approached the East Wing, out of the shadows emerged five figures dressed all in black with red bandanas covering the lower half of their faces. They took up positions in our path, striking what they probably thought were threatening poses. The biggest one spoke, affecting a growl that he had to have practiced.

"Well, look guys, it's two trash bags!"

As I was asking myself when "trash bags" became bully-lingo, Xander leaned over and whispered in my ear, "Daniel... That's Team Bulldog.

They're a gang of athletes at our school that thinks they're better than everyone. Even you."

"So, what are you two losers doing here anyway?" Team Bulldog #1 growled. He took one step toward us and the other four followed, reverting to their poses from before.

When we both stood our ground and remained silent, Team Bulldog #2, a girl, tried to growl but it came out more like clearing her throat. "He asked you a question, losers. And he does NOT like to be ignored!"

Acting as though I had only just realized that any of these kids had said anything to us, I tried to warn them nicely. "Look, guys – and girls — I'm sorry, but you don't know who you're messing with. Please back off."

Team Bulldog #1 shoved his "team" aside and took a step forward. His growl cracked (like my singing voice) as he said, "I think we're messing with a bunch of weak little kids like you."

Xander and I looked at each other and laughed, throwing Team Bulldog into confusion.

"You're LAUGHING at us, you jerks?!" Team Bulldog #2 screeched, peering from behind her leader's left shoulder.

Xander broke his silence. "We're just... *amused*...because you are picking on the leader of Team Triassic," he said, almost unable to get the words out because he was laughing so hard.

They all jumped back, with cries of "Whhhaaat!" "NO!" Two of the gang looked over their shoulders, maybe for an escape route?

"I don't buy it," Team Bulldog #2 said, recovering her bold stance.

From the back of the pack came another voice. "Yeah, what she said. We don't buy it at all."

Team Bulldog #1 took charge then. He whistled through his teeth and his team morphed into their *Velociraptor* forms. They raised their arms, baring their claws... but the tallest of them was only six feet in height.

Xander's natural reaction was to recoil in fear – after, all, these were the same sort of dino hybrids responsible for the attack on his mother and him. But then he looked at me a second and a change came over him. He dropped his backpack and put his hands up in a martial arts stance and stood there, glowering.

It looked like a stand-off that would not teach this dino hybrid gang a lesson, so I motioned Xander to take a few steps back. I morphed to a 25%

extension of my *Regem Insuperabilus* and roared right in their faces. At first they seemed paralyzed with shock. Then they turned on their heels and ran away at top speed, bumping into each other – probably out of sheer terror.

I shouted after them, "If I hear that you are picking on this kid — or any other kids — at school, you won't just be running away. You'll see what I can REALLY do to you!"

De-morphing, I said calmly, "So… where were we when we were so rudely interrupted?"

Xander couldn't answer at first because he was still laughing hard. As he picked up his backpack, he could finally speak.

"Dude! That was awesome!" he said with so much energy.

I nodded. "Yeah. Well, they will remember you for sure," I said, laughing. "Now, let's get you home, ok?"

I checked my holo as I left Xander's house and saw that I was scheduled to spar with Nick in twenty minutes, so I morphed to 25% to make it back to Lone Mountain in time. My *Regem Insuprabilus* slid to a halt at the doors to the gym with four minutes to spare. At 25% I could fit through the gym doors easily; but I immediately morphed to full extension when I saw Nick's *Regem Insuprabilus* waiting for me across the gym.

It is important for people to know that the object of our sparring matches was to *practice* maneuvers we would need to use against real adversaries, NOT to inflict pain or injury on each other. This meant that we "pulled our claws" and bit "gently," but realistically enough so the dino we were fighting could respond to such a maneuver as though it had been a full-on attack. From the sidelines, our matches looked real enough; but it was unusual for blood to be drawn or lasting injuries to be suffered. Of course, we all tolerated aches and pains after sparring, just as sports athletes have always done.

Kayla and Juli must have noticed my arrival, because right away the flashing lights and beep-beep-beep of the gym's warning system indicated the floor surface was about to change, and anyone in the gym needed to get to the perimeter where the Overseers generally sat. After a pause, the rumbling under the floor began and the Desert & Mountains configuration took shape. Two quick beeps signaled that the gym was ready for a sparring match.

If I didn't know better, I could have been looking in the mirror, instead of facing a sparring partner. Nick's *Regem Insuprabilus* was nearly identical to my own. Both of us were over eighteen feet tall with egg-shaped skulls like a *Giganotosaurus* but with oversized horns of both the *Allosaurus* and *Carnotaurus*, which gave us a very formidable look. Adding to the scary appearance were pyramid-like spikes from our head to tail tip that were set on plates similar to those of the *Anklosaurus*. A cyan blue stripe ran along the bottom of the plates above Nick's gray belly; on me this stripe was crimson over my gray belly. Both of us had *Velociraptor* arms with claws like the *Therizinosaurus* and *T-Rex* feet, which were suited for running on two legs at speeds up to twenty-two miles an hour.

This meant that the only difference between us –Nick's cyan blue stripe of scales – was not readily noticeable from across the gym. So it could look as though I was getting ready to spar against myself!

Lynnelle and Michael took their positions as Overseers. Then Elliott gave us the "SPARRERS READY… SET… GO!" signal and the match was on.

Nick tapped his raptor talon on the floor, signaling he was READY. We spent the first five-minute period sparring pretty evenly, with each of us earning three points, but I was disappointed because the battle wasn't really much of a challenge for either of us. The second period was much the same. During the rest before the last period, I looked over at Nick and saw that he was doing some major deep-breathing exercises and puffing himself up. Obviously, he wanted the final period to be more "realistic." Well, I was ready for that!

He and I stared at each other, dead in the eyes. At the bell, we each roared and charged in. I lunged the last five feet over a dune-like obstacle, grabbed hold of Nick, mock-biting his neck before pushing him back. He launched himself back toward me, forearms raised to press against my chest, flinging me back. My right foot hit a large rock, causing me to lose my balance and I tumbled to the ground.

With this great advantage, Nick charged in, probably planning to mock-bite me on the top side of my neck. But he bit too low, giving me the opportunity to wrap my head around and bite his neck with a little force. He backed off then and let out a little growl. I quickly pushed myself off the ground and whacked the left side of his head with my own head, lifting him up off the ground. He flew nearly twenty feet – over one of the low hills – and landed with a thunderous THUD on a sand dune, crushing it.

After a few seconds, he lifted his head up, shaking it. I could see that my last blow had caught him off guard. As I walked over to him slowly and placed one hand on his ribs and the other on the back of his head, he surrendered the match by tapping his claws on the ground. I released him and de-morphed. When Nick de-morphed, he was still lying on the ground.

Propping himself up on an elbow, he looked over at me. "Dude, I did NOT see that coming," he said with a little quiver in his voice.

"Well, you're not supposed to," I said, and if it came out harshly, that's not how I meant it. "You've got to be ready for anything," I said, in a kinder tone. I walked over to him and helped him up.

Still trying to shake off the effects of our match, he said, "I guess I was still using my *Velociraptor* senses. I'm not used to being so big." He gave a little embarrassed laugh.

It occurred to me then that this had been Nick's first sparring match against me, his "power equal." Earlier matches since he became a *Regem Insuprabilus* had been against Team members with battle skills and powers, but none of them were "unbeatable kings," as we were. Nick was only a few weeks into life as his new dino hybrid. *Should I have gone easy on him?* I asked myself.

I apologized to Nick then for being too aggressive in our very first match as "equals." He smiled and placed his hand on my shoulder.

"Hey, it's ok. Don't beat yourself up over it. I'll get you next time!" he said with a wink. I smiled at him and gave him and one-arm hug, with our usual fist-bump-blowup that meant "Thanks!"

We walked to the gym perimeter as the control room warned us the floor would be returning to flat canvas. Lynnelle and Michael passed us, saying, "Great match, guys!" almost in unison. We were near our office door when I got a sudden inspiration.

"Hey, Nick, why don't you ask if you could spend the night at my place?" I said. "It's been awhile since we spent time together outside of work here on the mountain."

"Heck yeah, man," he said as his face broke into a big grin. "It's been

WAY too long since we were just Daniel and Nick, ordinary Las Vegas teenagers. And the timing is right, I guess."

When I looked up at him after that last comment, he hurried to ask, "Too cold for the pool?

"Yeah, Bro… How about a game of HORSE on our new b-ball court?"

"Sounds like a plan," he said, pretending to dribble and let fly an imaginary jump-ball. "Swish!"

We both got on our holo-phones to our Moms. In less than two minutes, we gave each other thumbs up, and soon afterward we were off toward Nick's house so he could pick up what he'd need for a sleepover.

"Let's go!" I said. As we jogged out of Headquarters, we both had the same idea: SAVE TIME! Simultaneously, we morphed into our 25% *Regem Insuperabilus* hybrids, and in less than five minutes, we slid to a halt outside Nick's front door and de-morphed.

It had been quite a while since I had been at Nick's house, I realized, and I could see that their living room had undergone some changes... Actually, it now had a lot less furniture than I remembered. I knew that Nick's Mom was a pretty talented interior designer, and that got me to thinking: *Is Mrs. Williamson's going "minimalist?"* I followed Nick through the house to the stairs leading to the bedroom floor.

"Mom's probably in the kitchen, Daniel. She'll want to see you. Go ahead... I gotta get my stuff," he said, heading up the stairs. I turned right through the dining room to get to the kitchen.

Mrs. Williamson was coming back inside from the patio as I came through the dining room doorway. When she caught sight of me, the biggest smile grew on her face. She put down the platter she was carrying and sped over to sweep me into a big hug (with a peck on my cheek, too).

"Daniel, it's been a long time!" she said, holding me at arm's length. "Let me get a good look at you."

She tilted her head this way and that, assessing me from head to toe, then nodded her head once and said, "You look GREAT... Your scars are hardly noticeable! We've all missed you. Even Nick says you two work in the same building but don't spend enough down-time together anymore."

She stopped and thought for a minute, then added, "Well, maybe that's for the best..." She turned away and picked up the platter, keeping her back to me as she walked into the dining room.

What did she mean by that? I wondered. But the question faded because just then Nick's Dad came through the patio door carrying a hammer. When he saw me, he switched the hammer to his left hand, strode across the kitchen and put out his right for a handshake.

"Good to see you again, Daniel. You're just in time!" he said.

Nick's Mom had come back into the kitchen just then. She stepped between her husband and me, putting her hands on her hips as she gave him "a look."

"Nick is spending the night at Daniel's," she said. *"Just like the old days."* She stood there staring at her husband until he got whatever unspoken message she wanted him to get.

"Oh, yeah, that's probably a good idea because…" Nick's Dad began, then changed direction when his wife shook her head. "Yeah… just like the old days…" He turned around abruptly and went back out into the yard without another word.

I was so confused! But then Nick was standing in the door to the hallway, backpack ready to go. "Let's head out," he said. "Bye, Mom! Tell Dad I said bye… and Angel. See you tomorrow!"

His Mom blew him a kiss, which he "caught" and tapped to his heart, blowing her one back – which she caught and put into her heart. It was a sweet family thing they had always done, but this time I could swear Nick's Mom had a tear in her eye.

What is going on here?

Since one of the city's "No Dino Zones" spread out between Nick's house and ours, we had to walk over halfway to my house. I put up with no conversation from Nick for about the first five minutes. Then I couldn't stand it any longer.

I stopped walking and turned to block his path. "What is going on with your family?" I asked with a pleading look.

"What do you mean?" he asked innocently.

"There's something happening. Your parents seem… different. Your house doesn't look like it used to. What is going on?"

Nick hesitated for a long moment. Finally, he said, "It's a family thing, Daniel. I don't want to talk about it right now. Please… Can we just have fun together? Just this once?" He looked so pitiful that I had a flashback to that afternoon long ago after his grandmother died and he was so, so sad.

I didn't understand it, but I figured he'd tell me what was going on when he could.

"OK, Bro, sure… whatever you need…" I flung my arm around his shoulders – just like that other time – and we walked the rest of the way talking about other things.

"So… tell me about this prank war with Lynnelle," I began, and then we went from one thing to another, just catching each other up on "stuff." Before we knew it, we were opening the door to my house.

As he set his backpack down in the hallway, Nick said, "Wow, it's been awhile since I've been here."

"Yeah, it has," I agreed. "But nothing has changed here, though." The minute the words were out of my mouth, I realized that Nick was probably taking my comment the wrong way. After all, a lot seemed to be changing at *his* house.

Thankfully, Nick seemed not to have heard my last few words – or he chose to ignore them. In any case, the moment passed and we walked into the great room, where Andy was leaning over the kitchen counter talking to Mom.

Andy turned his head, caught sight of Nick, and joked, "Mom, what's going on? You'll let *anyone* in here these days!"

Mom laughed lightly, then came around the counter to hug Nick. "You are *always* welcome here, Nick," she said. "We missed you! Don't pay any attention to my rude son!"

Andy looked fake-shocked. "Me? Rude? Whatever do you mean?" he cried, grabbing Nick away from Mom's hug and messing up his hair playfully. "So what're you guys up to?"

"We're going to shoot some hoops," I said. "And YOU are not invited," I told my brother in a teasing tone, but I really didn't want him with us this afternoon – just in case Nick wanted to fill me in on his "family thing."

Upstairs, we dumped Nick's backpack and I changed into my favorite high-top basketball shoes. As we came down the stairs, Nick said, "Dude, it's so weird being here."

"Yeah. Well, it's been awhile," I said. "Ever since we've been so focused on Team Triassic training, we seem to have lost the 'old us.' I miss 'us,'" I said, and I really meant it.

We got the basketball out of the storage shed and Nick dribbled across the patio to our half-court basketball set-up, leaping high for an easy lay-up. I ran under the basket and snagged the rebound.

"Wanna play HORSE?" I asked, dribbling back toward the foul line.

"Sure!" Nick said. "You're first."

I started off with my "best" shot – from the foul line. Swish! Nick's foul shot caught the rim and circled around before falling off on the right side.

"That's an H for you," I said, heading to the left corner of the 3-point circle, my second-favorite shot. With great confidence, I launched an arcing ball that went... right over the basket.

"Air ball!" Nick called, gleefully. He took up his position in the opposite corner, dribbled once before flinging a perfect shot. Swish!

When I surprised myself by missing my shot from his corner, we were tied, an H apiece. Over the next twenty minutes or so, the score went back and forth, as we each tried our "best" shots to outdo the other. We were tied at H-O-R-S when Nick strode two-thirds of the way to the half-court line and turned around. With his back to the basket, he flung the ball hard, high over his head in a beautiful arc... that dropped into the net without a sound.

"Your turn, Bro," he said to me with the biggest grin ever.

I knew I was toast, but I gave it a try. I paced off the distance to the half-court line, dribbled about ten times (I was stalling), and tossed the ball over my head with all my might. The ball sailed past the backboard and disappeared over the wall into our neighbor's yard.

"Well, you win for distance!" Nick said, snickering. "But that still gives you an E. I win!"

At that very moment, my basketball came flying back over the wall, arcing over the backboard and dropping through the net for a perfect shot.

"Thanks, Mr. Kennedy," I shouted to my unseen neighbor. "You made a basket!"

"You're welcome, Daniel," a *female* voice replied. I looked at Nick with my mouth hanging open. *Mrs.* Kennedy was our ace-shooter!

"Is your neighbor with the WBA?" Nick whispered, only half-seriously.

"The Women's Basketball Association? No," I said. "And she's over fifty!"

Soon we were both laughing hysterically.

"Dude, I missed these days so much!" Nick said.

"Same here," I agreed.

A shadow crossed Nick's face for a second, but he shook it off and dribbled the ball back to the storage shed. I got us each a Dr. Pepper out of the patio fridge and we pulled up lounge chairs next to the drought garden.

After a few quiet minutes sipping our drinks, Nick turned toward me and asked in a surprisingly serious tone, "Daniel, what's your dream place to live?"

I had never really thought about that. After all, I'd lived in Las Vegas my whole life!

"I don't really know," I said. I put my lips together in a "thinking" pose, then said, "Probably in the mountains in the East. Why do you ask?"

"I was just wondering," he said. No explanation.

"Well, where would *you* want to live?" I asked.

Instantly, he said, "Near the ocean."

"Which one?" I asked.

"I don't know, either one. Sometimes things just happen, you know," Nick said.

I wasn't sure of what Nick meant by that. Before I could say anything, he got up and walked over to check one of Dad's hummingbird feeders. He ducked suddenly when a very aggressive red and green bird buzzed him.

"Whoa!" he shouted, retreating to his lounge chair as the hummingbird perched on the feeder and took a good, long drink.

"Yikes," he said. "I never knew they were like that. They're so little!" He took a long sip of his Dr. Pepper, sighed, sighed again and then looked right at me.

So… What do you think of Xander?" he asked, obviously bringing up a subject that had been on his mind.

"He's a great kid. He'll change a lot on the Team, like it's changed all of us," I said.

I knew that forming the Team *did* change us all. "Not long ago, we were just kids, but now people are calling us the Protectors of Las Vegas," I said. "It's an awesome responsibility and we CANNOT screw it up!"

"Well, *you're* the real Protector, actually. You saved me," Nick said.

"I know, but you'll have your opportunity someday soon, I think. It's been a long time since that rogue dino attack. Another attack has to be in the works," I said, with a warning tone.

"Anything can change things," he said and there was a real sadness in his voice.

Right then we heard, "Dinner in five minutes!" It was Mom's voice coming through the open patio door.

Another missed opportunity to learn about the "family thing," I thought.

Nick and I stood up just as Andy came around the corner from our side patio carrying a large platter. I held the patio door for him. Once inside, he gestured to Nick and me to get to the table, where Mom was already seated. I realized that he wanted to make "an entrance," so we took our seats.

Holding the large platter aloft, he intoned, "And to top dinner off tonight, I present to you freshly grilled ribs," setting the platter down with a flourish. We were just passing around the serving dishes when Dad walked through the door, taking off his lab coat and tossing it over the back of an extra chair.

"Hey, sorry I'm home so late. I got really into my research," he said, sitting down and grabbing for the ribs platter. It was more than a minute before he noticed the "extra" person at the table.

"Oh, hi, Nick. Didn't see you. Are you here for dinner?"

Dad is a genius, but sometimes he says things that make us all crack up. This was one of those times.

The next morning, I woke up to see Nick leaning on his elbow on the bed across the room, staring at me.

"I was wondering if you were ever going to wake up," he said. "It's almost seven. And it's our day off. Time for an adventure!"

"What kind of an adventure?" I asked. "Isn't Team Triassic 'adventure' enough?"

"Nope!" he said. "Get dressed for ACTION. Wear your fastest running shoes!"

He flipped the covers down and I saw that he was completely dressed, Nikes and all.

"Hurry up! I'll ask your Mom for a couple of Hot Pockets, some chips and water bottles. Meet you downstairs in five! We don't want to miss it." He dashed through the door and was gone before I could ask, "Miss what?!"

When I got downstairs, I asked, "Miss WHAT?"

"The train!" and he was off, running.

We jogged down the street to the open area behind our housing development. Closer to Xander's house off in the distance, I saw a train moving slowly on the tracks. Nick sped up, running a diagonal path to close the gap between us and the tracks quickly. I hustled up to try to stay with him.

Over his shoulder, Nick shouted, "We're going to jump into one of those box cars and go on a little trip!"

"*You've got to be kidding me!*" I thought, soon running at my top human speed. It was more than a quarter-mile to the tracks and Nick was at least fifty yards ahead of me. He kept yelling over his shoulder to me to "Keep up!"

I was so out of breath, though, that I couldn't say anything. I just kept running, trying to catch up with him.

As we came alongside the slow-moving train, we kept pace with it for about a hundred feet, finding just the right boxcar – one with a wide-open door, of course – to jump into. Nick leaped aboard with no problem. He held his hand out to help me, but I still had to run almost another hundred feet before I could get up the nerve to make the jump. *For crying out loud,* I thought. *I fought a SpinoRex, but I don't have the nerve to jump aboard a slow-moving train!*

Once aboard, I saw that Nick had sat down on a little crate. "Have a seat Daniel," he said with a smile on his face, kicking a little crate in front of him. I sat down on the crate and looked at him. "So where are we going?" I asked.

He looked at me with the biggest smile on his face. "I'm taking you to see my favorite spot to view Las Vegas. It's up on Mt. Charleston. It'll take us about thirty minutes to get there," he said.

I was actually happy that he was taking me to Mt. Charleston, since I'd never been there. He looked out the door as the train was moving faster. He closed his eyes and breathed in the nice, cool air as it rushed past us.

"Ahhh, I just love to sit in these box cars, feeling the breeze as we go to the top of the mountain," he said.

"Do you do this often?" I asked, wondering why I had known Nick for almost four years and never knew about his train-jumping.

"Yeah, it's something Angel taught me. We do it together whenever we can… more often since you helped us understand each other, actually," he said, nodding to me.

"Well, thanks for taking me today," I said. "The breeze feels nice. And I always wanted to see what's on Mt. Charleston. What IS up there, anyway?"

Nick faced me. "Well, there's the train station, a ski resort, and a cottage, but we'll be getting off the train before it reaches the station," he said.

I nodded my head and looked out the door as we rode higher. The temperature dropped quite a lot the higher we rode. Soon I started seeing things we never saw in the Las Vegas valley – deciduous trees and bushes and hundreds of pine trees. The leaves were "painted" with the widest variety of reds, golds, oranges and some brilliant crimsons that shone in the sun, the dark green of the pines providing the perfect backdrop. Here and there we could see little patches of snow. It was beautiful!

"Look, Nick!" I shouted, suddenly catching sight of two does and a fawn. *Wow, this is paradise,* I thought to myself, daydreaming.

"Are you feeling cold?" Nick asked, bringing my mind back to the boxcar.

I rubbed my arms. "A little bit, but I'm fine," I said.

"All right, good, 'cause we're getting off here really soon," he said, standing up. He walked over to the door and leaned out, holding on with one arm.

"How soon?" I asked. He looked back in, then back out. "In about... 30 seconds," he shouted.

"Are we going to JUMP OFF this train??" I screamed. "Isn't it going to STOP somewhere?"

He came over and knelt in front of me. "Yep, we're going to jump," he said. "Here is how you jump off the train without getting hurt. You jump, land on your feet, but roll as you fall. Got it?" he asked.

I looked at him as if he were some crazy human being. "Uh, yeah, I got it," I said, with a VERY shaky voice.

"Don't be scared. I'll go first. Watch how I do it," he said.

I stood up and got behind him as he got ready to jump. Next thing I knew, he lunged forward and leaped out of the train. He landed on his feet and rolled forward on the ground.

"OK Daniel! JUMP!" He yelled as the train moved farther away from him. I put no thought into what I was doing and just jumped.

Chapter 21

"Daniel! DANIEL! Are you OK?" Nick was leaning over me, patting my cheeks.

I looked around at a blurry landscape. "Wh-where am I?"

"We're on Mt. Charleston," Nick said. "You just did a GREAT jump-and-roll off the train!"

My head was pounding, my vision was blurry and I was confused. "What train?" I asked. I shook my head, trying to clear both my vision and my brain. "I *jumped off* a train?!" I cried. At that moment, Dr. Lingard's warning from last year popped into my aching head:

"Keep in mind, Daniel, that you will always be susceptible to concussions and other head injuries because your brain has experienced coma," he had told me in one of our one-on-one chats after I woke up. "You may experience problems if you hit your head, so be careful!"

I just sat there on the ground in the middle of a snowbank, blinking my eyes again and again, straining to return my vision to normal. My glasses had remained in place during my ill-advised jump (Surprise!), so I should have been able to see perfectly. But things were still out of focus. I closed my eyes.

"Daniel, what can I do to help you?" Nick asked in a shaky voice, leaning close to me, pushing snow off me. "Do I need to call somebody?"

"Just let me lie down for a minute," I said.

He quickly cleared the ground behind me and guided me into a reclining position with his arm, gathering some soft leaves together for a "pillow."

Lying down seemed to do the trick. My headache went away almost immediately and when I opened my eyes a few minutes later, my vision had returned to normal. The multi-colored blur of a few minutes ago was now a beautiful landscape of trees and bushes, all dressed for autumn.

"Hey, I think I'm ok," I said, sitting up easily.

"You sure?" Nick asked, moving beside me, ready to catch me if I keeled over, I think.

"Yep!" I said. "So… remind me… why are we here?" Nick put a hand under my elbow and I stood up.

"You're SURE you're ok?" Nick asked, looking me directly in my eyes.

"YES I AM," I said firmly. "Now, what's the plan?"

He looked at me again, probably still not sure I wouldn't collapse, but then he said, "OK. If you're up to it… Come on, I want to show you something."

I brushed the twigs, leaves and dirt off my jeans as I followed him a few hundred feet into a stand of trees. We walked along a rough snow-covered path for another thousand yards or more before we passed through a thicket and I caught sight of a very old tree house about ten feet up in the space between two Ponderosa pines. Nick grabbed a makeshift ladder conveniently left nearby, propped it against the pine and started up.

With my recent head trauma still in mind, I hesitated at the bottom of the ladder.

"Nick, are you sure this is safe?" I asked.

He looked down at me and laughed. "Dude, I've been up here tons of times. It's safe," he said, with a "C'mon" gesture.

I took his word for it and started my way up. The ladder creaked loudly at the halfway point and I froze. I held onto the ladder for dear life and looked up at Nick.

"Dude, come on! It's safe. It's a wood ladder that always does that," he said, in his most "reassuring" tone.

Realizing I had five feet to go either way, I decided to go on up.

"Ok…" I said, and I took a deep breath.

I made my way to the top of the ladder quickly, spending only a second or two on each rung – in case it would give way, I guess. Then I was at the door of the treehouse. I ducked my head and stepped inside, where I could actually stand up. Across from the door was a huge "window" – no glass, of course – that looked out on an amazing view of the entire Las Vegas valley. A cool, light cross-breeze wafted from the window to the door.

"So, this is what you wanted to show me, huh?" I asked.

Nick leaned over the edge of the open window and gestured that I should do so, too. He looked over at me and nodded his head. I looked out at the valley.

"Wow, it's so… peaceful," I said.

"It's a place to relieve stress for me. Angel and I found this ten years ago… Well, Angel actually discovered it and brought me along, 'cause I was still little. We think somebody must have built it before this became BLM land, but we've never seen evidence that anyone else has been here since we found it. It was perfect for us. We wanted a place to get away from – from…" He hesitated a second, then continued, "from *everything*. Angel doesn't come up here much anymore, so now it's just a place for me to relax," he said softly.

"It's amazing up here," I said sincerely. "Thanks for bringing me here."

Nick looked me in my eyes. He took a deep breath. "There's another reason why I brought you up here…" Nick began, then stopped.

"What is it?" I asked. Immediately, I remembered he had said there was a "family thing" going on and a feeling of dread settled on me.

A sadness came over his face and he looked down at the floor.

"Nick, look at me," I said, reaching over to raise his chin with two fingers. "You know you can tell me anything… right?" I said.

He nodded his head, "I- I know. I just never told this to anyone…" he said, and he took another deep breath.

"Not *anyone?*" I asked.

"No, not even my Mom or Dad or Angel. It's a pretty big secret, and I want to know if I can trust you with it," Nick said, his voice cracking, and he looked down again.

Now I was scared. What could it be? Was he sick? In trouble? What kind of "family thing" would be a secret from… from his *family?*

"You can trust me. I won't tell a soul," I said.

Nick took another deep breath. He put his hand over his mouth and a tear dropped out of his eye. In a very dry voice, he began, "I'm… I'm…"

I nodded, encouraging him to go on.

Nick looked out the window and said in a voice just above a whisper, "I- I'm gay and... I'm scared that you won't accept me for who I am and you won't want to be friends anymore..." he said, turning to look me with fear in his eyes.

I jumped a little. I had *not* expected him to say that. We looked at each other steadily.

"How long have you felt this way?" I asked, after a few seconds.

"A long time," he said. "Years." He looked at me steadily. "Does it change how you feel about me... as a friend? Or as part of Team Triassic?" he asked, with worry in his voice.

It seemed a little strange to me that I had never seen even a hint of this part of Nick before. But this was a time for support, not questioning.

I scooted a little closer to him on the bench and flung my arm over his shoulders. "Does it change things? No, no! Don't even think that! This won't change anything in our friendship. We have been best friends – like brothers — for a long time, and Team Co-Leaders for over a year," I said, looking him full in the face. "You are still the same person you have always been. Nothing has changed between us today, and it never will," I said and I was 100% sincere.

Nick looked like he was about to break down. "Thank you," he said quietly.

I gripped his shoulder tighter, then released it. "You're still my brother-from-another-mother," I said, sitting back and ruffling his hair in a playful gesture — to lighten the mood a little.

Nick got the hint, smoothed his hair, and whined, "Aw, now I need a mirror!"

Looking around the treehouse, seeing nothing that resembled a mirror, I gave Nick the good news: "Bro, it's probably better that you *don't* see what you look like right now."

"You, too!" he laughed. He messed up my hair, and then we were scooping up dried pine needles and tossing them at each other, "fencing" with fallen pine branches and simply *playing*.

This is the kind of fun that we brothers need to have more often, I thought. We both probably looked a sight a few minutes later as we climbed down the ladder, but I knew that this was a good day for both of us.

"Hey, Nick, I really appreciate you showing me your treehouse and trusting me," I said, as we headed out of the forest.

"Well, you *are* like my brother, y'know," he said. "C'mon... the train will be heading down the mountain in a few... Time to hop on!"

I stopped dead in my tracks. He turned around and came back to me.

"No worry...," he said, reassuringly. "It comes to a complete stop about four hundred yards from where we hopped on earlier. No need to jump off this time!"

Relieved at this news, I jogged to catch up.

Getting on the train this time was a snap, since I was now a "veteran" of this semi-extreme sport. We rode along, mostly in silence, relaxing against a couple of sacks of grain. As we were approaching the outskirts of the city, I broke the silence to ask a question that had been on my mind ever since we were at the tree house. I sat up.

"Hey, Bro," I began. "I'm just wondering how Lynnelle fits into what you told me this afternoon."

He propped himself up on an elbow and looked at me with some confusion. "What do you mean?"

"Well, all this pranking that the two of you have been doing... Lots of times that sort of thing is just a 'cover' for feelings two people have for each other."

"Nah, it's only pranking," he said. "We don't mean anything by it. It's just for fun."

I didn't know that I agreed with Nick. I said, "I've seen how she looks at you, Nick. She likes you... a LOT. It's obvious the pranks are a way she can get your attention."

"Nah," he insisted. "Lynnelle is like my sister... She's like a 'sister-from-another-moth...'" He stopped. "Oh, wait – That doesn't rhyme."

"I know," I said. Then with sudden inspiration, I cried, "She's a 'sister-from-another-*mister!*'" I cracked up at my cleverness.

"A-sister-from-another-mister! That's *perfect*," Nick said, high-fiving me with a handshake and blow-up. "I'll tell her tomorrow!"

I wasn't so sure that Lynnelle would be thrilled about her status as Nick's 'sister,' but it wasn't my business.

Chapter 22

The train came to a stop and we hopped off with no problems, just as my holo buzzed with an audio reminder from Elliott.

In his usual stern tone, Elliott said, "DANIEL, PLEASE MAKE YOUR WAY TO YOUR APPOINTMENT WITH MR. MARTINEZ AT MOLASKY MIDDLE SCHOOL. YOU ARE SCHEDULED TO MEET IN HIS OFFICE IN EXACTLY SEVENTEEN MINUTES. DO NOT BE LATE!"

"OMG," I said to Nick. "Our Mt. Charleston adventure almost made me forget about this meeting."

"What's it about?" Nick asked.

"I really don't know," I told him. "But he said I could bring any of the Team along if I wanted. Wanna come?"

"Sure!" Nick said. "But we better morph at 25% to get there in time."

"Good idea," I agreed, as I took in a deep breath — so did Nick – and our two *Regem Insuperabilus* hybrids delivered us to Molasky in less than nine minutes flat.

We were just de-morphing outside the school's front door when we saw Mr. Martinez holding the door open for us. "Whew, guys, your dinos could have shaken the whole school!" he said, jokingly.

He motioned us inside, continuing to chat away. "It's been awhile since anyone saw you in your live dino form, Daniel... and now there are TWO of you?"

"Ha, sorry, Mr. Martinez," I said sincerely, shaking his hand. "We didn't mean to scare you. You remember Nick, don't you?"

"Of course!" he said, reaching out to shake hands with Nick. "You are probably the one person other than Daniel who *should* be here today," he said.

Nick and I looked at each other, puzzled.

"Why?" I asked Mr. Martinez.

"You'll see. Come with me," he said as he walked away from us down the hallway.

As we followed the principal, Nick and I pointed out rooms we each remembered. "This place holds so many memories," Nick said. I agreed.

Mr. Martinez ducked his head in the Teachers' Lounge door and said, "It's time." As Nick and I passed that room, we were joined by Mrs. Johnson, Mrs. Hollis, Coach Hitchcock, Mrs. Leeper and some other teachers I didn't recognize. Everybody greeted us like we were old friends, then fell in behind us as we all followed Mr. Martinez.

Our group came to a stop when Mr. Martinez reached out to open the large, brand-new glass door to the quad.

"Come on, everyone," he said and stepped inside, walking to the quad center where something huge was covered by a tarp.

He motioned that we should encircle this thing. When we were in place, Mr. Martinez cleared his throat, flipped the inter-school Holo-Camera recording system to "ON," and began what were obviously prepared remarks that would be beamed into all classrooms on the next school day.

"All Molasky teachers, staff and students, please give me your attention. Today is a very special day here at our school. As you all know, disaster struck this school a little over a year ago when we were attacked by a rogue dinosaur whose goal was death and destruction. If it had not been for this young man here" – he reached out to pull me into the 'picture' — "I simply cannot imagine what that day would have brought to Molasky. You all know Daniel Robertson. He saved everyone in this school from what might have been serious injury or even death. We also have with us today the young man Daniel saved from the claws – or the jaws — of that *Spinosaurus Rex*, Nick Williamson."

He motioned for Nick to join us in the 'picture.' Looking very embarrassed, Nick ducked his head and shuffled next to me.

Mr. Martinez reached over and patted Nick on his back, then continued, "All of us at Molasky are forever grateful to Daniel for saving us then and we have been thankful since that day for Team Triassic, assembled by Daniel and Nick. For these reasons, we have created a 'little something' to remember that day at Molasky."

He grabbed the tarp with his right hand and pulled hard. As the tarp dropped, we saw a life-size statue of my *Regem Insuperabilus* hovering over the dying *Spinosaurus Rex*, my right leg pressed down on the beast's ribs. It was clear that Mr. Martinez was very proud of this addition to the quad.

I really appreciated the gesture, but, to tell the truth, it bothered me a bit that what the statue showed *never happened*. I never pinned down the *SpinoRex*, and the gash on my leg – that almost killed me – was nowhere to be seen.

When I looked tentative, Mr. Martinez nudged me. He said, "Go on, read the plaque."

I walked up to it. The date-plaque read, *"On this day our school was attacked by a monster. Daniel Robertson's dino hybrid fought and killed this terrifying Spinosaurus Rex. This statue is in honor of Daniel, the young Molasky student who saved us all."*

Mr. Martinez walked up to me, "What do you think?" he asked.

I nodded my head, saying (without complete truth), "I think it's great! Thank you, Mr. Martinez… but it's really too much…"

"Not so, young man!" he said. "This is the least we could do!"

At that moment, Elliott started buzzing like crazy in my pocket.

Chapter 23

I probably should have mentioned before now that our Team shared "as needed" night shifts whenever our 24/7 city surveillance picked up evidence of a threatening situation we might need to handle. About a week before, there had been unusual activity in the No-Dino area near the Strip, so Xander, Juli and Kayla pulled an all-nighter, just keeping watch. Kayla was still singing "You Can't Get a Man with a Gun!" when she and Juli got to Headquarters after rehearsal. But they settled in to work right away, coordinating with Xander. Luckily, whatever creature it was that had triggered our warnings seemed to have lost interest in wrecking the city, moving off after causing minimal damage.

As was our practice in situations like this, Xander and Kayla just forwarded a Status Report to Elliott, who merely filed it for reference, as the threat had passed. This is the main reason that both Nick and I were blissfully unaware that this threat had happened during our sleepover and day on Mt. Charleston. Our Team had shown they and Elliott were all perfectly capable of handling a passing threat without having to get all of the rest of us involved. I am very proud of the capable Team I have on Lone Mountain!

As we left Molasky that day, however, I could tell that the threat was very real and it was going to need all of us. Elliott's message had sounded way more urgent than usual, as he barked, "DANIEL! NICK! THIS IS NOT A DRILL. GET BACK TO HEADQUARTERS IMMEDIATELY!"

He had faded from the screen as Juli's face faded in. She looked very worried.

"Remember that dino that Kayla, Xander and I were watching a few nights ago?" she asked, breathlessly. Before we could respond, she rushed on: "It was spotted eight minutes ago at the intersection of Durango and Centennial… and – unless there's something wrong with our sensors – it looks like there are TWO of them!"

Kayla was on-screen then, saying, "That's not the worst part… Here, I'll pull up the security feed."

Our eyes widened as a massive dino – and another one — appeared on-screen. As they came closer to the camera, I could see that both were genetically modified hybrids, but a type I had not seen before. They were over nineteen feet tall and generally resembled T-Rexes but with the enlarged, extra-hard skulls of a *Pachycephalosaurus.* Rows of armored plates ran down along their spines, similar to those of a *Nodosaurus*, ending in an eight-foot-long flexible tail. The two could have been twins, except that one's belly was black with purple markings under the armored plates; the other was brown-bellied with green markings.

As they lumbered along, the two beasts seemed to be having a serious issue with each other, growling back and forth and swatting at each other. As they approached the outskirts of the Centennial High School parking lot, I pulled my wristband Elliott close to get a better look, just in time to see the one with the purple markings turn suddenly, grab the other beast's head and pick the huge creature up off its feet. The aggressor held its adversary high in the air for a couple of seconds, then slammed it down. The ground shook from the force of the crash, but it was all over. The purple-marked creature roared in victory over its very dead "near-twin" and turned back toward the high school, just as my Elliott screen went black.

Elliott's text explained it: "DANIEL AND TEAM, HOLO-CAMERA NUMBER 46 HAS DIS-FUNCTIONED. IT APPEARS TO HAVE BEEN KNOCKED DOWN OR OTHERWISE DESTROYED."

Kayla's face faded in. "Our ground-sensors have been tracking these dinos. They are HUGE and heavier than any of us," she said, looking to the left where the sensor screens were located. She turned back to the camera again and there was real fear in her eyes.

"They're both at Centennial High School!" she cried. "Oh, wait

— One appears to be down. But the other one is crossing the parking lot toward the theater wing!"

At that moment, Nick, Elliott and I had exactly the same thought. Nick and I were already morphing to full extension, as Elliott's voice boomed to every Team Triassic receiver:

"CODE RED! CODE RED! TEAM TRIASSIC, MOBILIZE TO CENTENNIAL HIGH SCHOOL. MORPHING RESTRICTIONS ARE LIFTED. GO AT ONCE!"

Chapter 24

As Juli shouted orders, Elliott tracked each of us as we made our way to the high school. Juli sent in the flying dinos first for an overview of what we could expect. Within minutes, Andy had flown over from work and Timeer had joined him in the air a couple of blocks from the school, where the beast had already burst into the theater, leaving a huge hole in the brick wall.

On my wrist holo I saw Andy and Timeer swoop through the hole after the beast, diving at it and clawing at the top of its head. Juli kept re-positioning camera angles so Elliott could let all of the rest of us see what was happening. With perfect maneuvering, they kept swooping and diving, just to annoy and distract the beast from destroying everything – and every*one* – in its path, as the rest of us were getting there as fast as we could.

It was clear that this gigantic, violent beast was more dangerous than last year's *SpinoRex*, so it would take a Team effort to stop its rampage.

I shouted into my wrist-holo, "Juli, have Lynnelle ride on Matthew's back, so she can get to the school fast. We need to surround the theater building, so Lynnelle can set up a safe escape corridor for the kids while we deal with the beast inside."

"You got it, Daniel!" Juli responded within seconds. "Lynnelle, Matthew and Juli are en route, running at top speed with Johnny and Michael. Angel is on his way from across town."

A series of holos from inside the theater showed horrible sights of destruction and many, many injured kids. I was almost to the shattered wall of the theater when I suddenly remembered: Xander and his brother go to Centennial, and I think Xander said they both had Theater classes.

This realization was like a shot of adrenalin to me… I zoomed across the parking lot, just as Michael crashed through the hole in the wall, immediately jumping in the air, as if the beast was right in front of him. He roared, and a thunderous sound echoed back. These animal sounds joined with the ear-splitting noise of massive destruction inside the theater and the screams, wails and moans of the kids who were at the mercy of the rampaging dino hybrid. All hell was breaking loose inside the school!

I leaped through the broken wall, looked around frantically to come up with a battle plan. Matthew dashed across the room, leaping over fallen sections of the ceiling and pushing aside rows of broken seating. He did a "third-base slide" aimed at the beast's back legs to knock it off-balance. I could see that Andy and Michael were on its back, jabbing and biting it over and over, triggering the beast to swat at them and shudder… but only a little, unfortunately. Mostly unbothered, the beast kept reaching down, scooping up and flinging theater seats or pieces of rubble – it didn't seem to matter *what* he grabbed – as his main objective appeared to be hurling debris at the kids who were trying to hide or run away. His aim was deadly, as proven by more than a dozen kids who lay crumpled and bloody in the piles of rubble.

This is not an ordinary creature by any stretch of the imagination, I thought.

Taking advantage of the beast's preoccupation then with grabbing a fleeing kid, I charged at it in one powerful leap, sinking my serrated teeth into its neck. This got the beast's attention! It dropped the kid, whipped its head toward me, bellowed an ear-splitting roar and whacked me in the head with its own hard head. I reeled backward.

At the same time, the creature seemed to have had enough of Michael's annoyance. It shook Michael off, pounding him to the ground, then lowered its head to finish Michael off. The beast was within inches of squashing Michael when Nick charged in out of nowhere, his head down, and slammed into the dino hybrid's ribs with his horns, knocking it off balance and allowing Michael to dart up and perch on the stage-lighting bar. Andy flew away from the beast and perched next to Michael. The battle was now in the hands – or claws – of us large dino hybrids, so Andy and Michael could relax; they had done their part!

Down on the floor, the beast had shown its great power and flexibility as it flipped over onto its feet. It charged at Nick with its head down. Thankfully, it seemed to have lost sight of me, as I was positioned strategically over its left shoulder. But before it reached Nick, the beast grabbed a little girl in its teeth and flung her against a wall across the room. She slid down the wall like a ragdoll and was still. When the creature turned back to attack Nick, I seized my opportunity: I bit its tail to the bone. The beast roared in agony.

Using this to his advantage, Nick bit the right side of the dino hybrid's neck and began pulling him towards the hole in the wall. Johnny's *Ostrafrikasaurus* stepped through the hole and joined the struggle to get the resistant monster outside, in hopes of protecting any kids still in the theater. As I moved into position to help, I felt something running up my tail. It was Michael, using my scales as a staircase; then he launched himself into the air from my snout, flying twelve feet before landing on the beast's head and sinking his teeth in. Matthew charged in and went under the dino before lifting it up into the air on his back.

Together, we pulled the dino hybrid outside into the empty theater parking lot. As I cleared the broken masonry, I looked over my shoulder and saw that Lynnelle had ushered uninjured kids out the stage door, returning to search for kids who hadn't been so lucky.

Outside, the badly outnumbered invading beast was still not ready to give up the fight. I threw him onto the ground, but the beast got back up on its feet and roared at us, asking for more. It charged at me with its head down, but its aim was a little off this time. I quickly moved out of the way and slashed its face with my claws, knocking it down.

Nick placed his right foot on the dino hybrid's neck and roared into the afternoon sky. He looked at me, nodded his head down at the creature, telling me to finish it off. I leaned down, confidently placing my right hand on the beast's jaw and my left on the back of its head (the same move I used to finish off the *SpinoRex*). But when Nick let off some pressure, the beast flung its head into the air, breaking my grip and knocking Nick off-balance. The creature stood up, whirled around and bit Nick in the neck. Nick went down, hard. When I tried to get my death-grip back on the beast's head, I felt myself flung onto the ground.

I looked up and saw Angel's *Tyrannosaurus Rex* pushing the beast away from his brother, then slamming it into an unbroken section of the wall. The wall collapsed and so did the rogue dino hybrid. With an earthquake-like BOOM, it crumbled to the ground and was still. Angel placed his left foot on the creature's ribs, crushing them – for good measure — before roaring to the sky in victory.

For about three minutes, everybody was still, scanning the area, making sure the threat was really over. Then we all de-morphed and moved out of the way as police cars, ambulances and firetrucks jockeyed for position, screeching to a halt, and First Responders grabbed their gear.

Angel swaggered up to me, affecting a look of all innocence. "Take me too long?" he asked with a wink.

"Just in time," I said, still out of breath. "We needed all of us for this one. We did our best, but I'm afraid we have too many casualties inside."

"Not only inside," Matthew said, pointing.

I looked over at Nick, noticing for the first time that his neck was badly gashed.

"Oh dang, Nick — you should sit down," I said.

He shook his head no. "I'm fine. It only hurts a little," he said, as a steady river of blood ran down over his shoulder onto his chest.

I stepped next to Nick and placed my hand on his wound. "Oh yeah, that beast got you good," I said. "You're lucky, though… it missed your jugular."

When he jerked away from my hand, it was clear that my very light pressure was probably hurting him. I looked at my hand and it was covered in blood.

"Angel, you should get Nick to the Centennial Hills Hospital. If Dr. Lingard is there, you could ask for him. We go 'way back,'" I said, remembering. "We'll meet you there soon."

"All right. Come on, Nick. Let's go." Angel morphed and reached out to help his brother onto his back.

Nick hesitated. "No, really, I'm fine," he insisted.

I placed my hand on his shoulder, "Nick, please, don't fight us on this. Just get patched up. We have everything taken care of here," I said, pointing at the dozens of police cars, firetrucks and ambulances filing the theater parking lot.

He nodded his head, "Ok… Ok I'll- I'll go," he said.

I nodded my head. "Good. I'll meet you there soon."

Angel grabbed Nick's arm, swung him onto his back and they headed off to Centennial Hills Hospital. I walked over to Metro Chief Emerson to offer Team Triassic's help. As I waited for the Chief to finish the directions he was giving to his officers, Andy came up behind me.

"Hey, Daniel, you all right?" Andy asked, placing his hand on my shoulder.

I nodded my head. "Yeah, I'm fine. You ok?" His colorful scales looked a little ruffled, but he nodded, so I decided he was the right Team member for an important "errand" I just thought of.

"Those two were completely new dino hybrids. That means we need to get some blood and flesh samples for Dad to study… before they cart the carcasses away."

"How can I help?" Andy asked.

"We'll need syringes and sterile vials from Dad's lab. I'll get Elliott to get them ready for you. Stay morphed and get to the lab ASAP. I'll have Johnny and Timeer meet you at the first carcass in… about three minutes, ok? Johnny'll take the samples and you and Timeer can fly them up to Lone Mountain."

"Got it, Bro!" He was up and out of sight in seconds.

I filled Elliott in on all this, so he could coordinate with the lab and Johnny and Timeer.

Chief Emerson noticed me just then and reached out to shake my hand. I remembered that he had a reputation as a man of few words and lots of action, so I wasn't surprised when he just said, "Daniel, I'm heading inside to survey the damage and check casualties. Come with me."

Chapter 25

We climbed through the hole and over the rubble inside, making our way over piles of smashed concrete, twisted seating, rebar, pipes and broken ceiling tiles. We skirted around First Responders who were carefully pulling kids out from under piles of debris and removing the living to a sort of triage area on the stage, where EMT's and nurses were assessing their injuries. Matthew and Lynnelle were on the stage, too, where it appeared they had been asked to comfort the less-severely injured kids who had escaped life-threatening injury but who were traumatized, nevertheless, by the monster's attack. Their plaintive cries for "Mom!" "Mama!" and their missing friends and siblings were heart-breaking.

I was wondering how I could best be of help here, when I heard a kid call out from under a pile of broken ceiling tiles near the back of the auditorium. I made my way over to him, picking up a flat piece of metal on the way in case I had to pry rubble off him. He was trying to uncover himself by the time I got to him, so I helped free his blond head that was probably a mullet with buzz-cut sides, but at the moment it just looked like a bloody mess of dust, pieces of tile and dirt.

As I freed his upper body, I said, "Hi, I'm Daniel from Team Triassic. Are you hurt?"

"I – I don't know," he said. Pointing overhead, he explained, "I was up top working tech…"

I looked up at a big hole in the ceiling.

"That dinosaur came in and knocked everything all over the place. Then the floor gave out from under me... and here I am," he said simply.

"What's your name?" I asked, as I continued to remove debris from atop him.

"I'm Tucker," he said quietly. As I pushed aside a large piece of concrete, other pieces in the pile on him shifted.

"Ow, ow, OW!" he screamed, then he fainted.

I stood up and shouted, "Hey! Can I get some help over here?!" I flailed my arms to get someone's attention.

"Coming!" Matthew shouted as he zigzagged his way from the stage through the wrecked auditorium. He leaped the last few feet and squatted next to me.

"What's up?" he asked, breathless.

"Help me get this stuff off him," I said.

"All right," he said, reaching down and grabbing a big section of ceiling rafters.

"On three," I said.

He nodded his head.

"1... 2... 3!" We lifted two rafters off him. As I leaned over to get another very heavy piece of concrete off Tucker, it was suddenly lightweight, as two hands helped me lift it.

These weren't Matthew's hands. He was over near the back wall, standing up the rafters we had just removed. *The sun must be shining through a hole in the ceiling,* I thought, *because these helping hands have a soft glow.* When I looked up to see whose hands they were, I had to smile. It was Joseph! I hadn't had a visit from my "coma-buddy" in a year.

As I jumped back a little, shaking my head, Joseph smiled. In the kind voice I remembered so well, he said, "I'm still here with you, Daniel. When you need me, know that I am always just a wink away."

I wanted so badly to say something to Joseph, but I couldn't. Matthew was heading back toward me and I didn't want him – or anyone — to think I'm crazy.

Joseph nudged me then. "Come on, let's get all this off him," he said, bending down to shove away more debris. I knelt to help, just as Matthew was back. When I looked up again for Joseph, he was gone.

"Daniel... Daniel? Are you ok?" Matthew asked, looking me in the face.

I shook my head. "Uh- y- yeah. Sorry... I zoned out for a second," I said.

He looked at me and tilted his head with a confused look, then shrugged and went back to moving stuff off Tucker, who was now coming to and moaning softly. His color didn't look good.

"What do you think hurts?" I asked him.

"Uh- my legs... I think." He took a deep breath and exhaled slowly.

I picked up one piece of ceiling tile and my heart sank to my stomach. The left side of Tucker's abdomen was impaled by a broken water pipe. I touched it lightly to see if it was loose but it didn't budge. It appeared to be protruding from a piece of the ceiling that was under the kid, holding his body fast. Blood was oozing out around the pipe, pooling on the pile of rubble next to him.

When he saw the look on my face, Tucker strained to sit up enough to see what had upset me. Instinctively, he reached for the pipe, trying to pull it out.

"STOP!" I yelled at him. "Leave it where it is! I'm going to get somebody." I stood up and looked around wildly for somebody who could help. "HELP! HELP!" I called.

Two EMT's who were just returning from carrying a kid to an ambulance heard me and jogged over.

"What do we have here?" the red-headed female EMT asked, stooping down. Her male partner pulled out a blood pressure cuff and began wrapping it around Tucker's left arm. When they saw the position of the pipe, they looked at each other with worried faces. The red-head stood up, walked a little way off from us and spoke quietly into her wrist holo. When she returned, she looked grim; then she put on a smile for Tucker.

"Young man," she said, "we are going to take care of you, but you will have to be very brave." Spreading her hand to span the visible part of the pipe, she said, "I have called for someone to cut this part of the pipe away so we can move you to the ambulance. The hospital will be ready to operate on you the moment you arrive. Now, I am going to give you a shot that will relieve your pain. It will probably make you sleepy... which is not a bad thing, is it?"

"I- I gg-guess not," Tucker said. He looked at Matthew and me then. "Th-thanks, guys. Thanks for…" The shot must have kicked in then because his eyes closed.

"We'll take good care of him," the red-head said. "Thanks for calling us over. You probably saved his life."

Since Tucker was in good hands with the EMTs, I looked around the theater to see if there was any need for my help anywhere else. Diagonally across the ruined room there was a girl with dirty blonde hair who was propped like a ragdoll against the wall. I could see that she had a huge gash on her forehead that rained blood down her face, staining her white blouse.

I walked over to her. "Hey, you OK?" I asked.

She looked up at me, but her eyes looked unfocused. Slurring her words, she said, "Yeah, I- I think so. But my shoulder hurts a LOT." To show me, she touched her left shoulder with her right hand and winced.

"Do you think it's broken?" I asked, kneeling down and placing my hand on her shoulder very lightly. "Can you move your shoulder at all?" I asked.

She shook her head. "No, I can't feel it or move it," she said.

"Do you know how you got injured?" I asked.

She shivered, remembering. "That monster picked me up and threw me against the wall here. There wasn't anything I could do. I was so scared!"

"Well, you are safe now," I said. "I think your shoulder is just dislocated, but you'll need stitches on your forehead, I'm sure. By the way, I'm Daniel. What's your name?"

She looked at me steadily. "Aren't you the leader of Team Triassic?"

When I nodded, she wiped blood away from her eye, grinned weakly and said in a sing-songy voice, "Well, I'm Aurora and I'm not the leader of *anything.*"

Just then two EMTs came into the theater. I waved them over, introduced them to Aurora and left her in their care. I stood up to survey the room. A large Metro policeman was guarding the door to the Girls Dressing Room. I was just wondering why that room needed a guard when the door opened a little to let out a woman in an EMT uniform and I could see that there were several bodies covered in red blankets lined up on the floor of the Dressing Room. Oh no… a temporary morgue. The body nearest the door was obviously that of a petite girl. Sticking out from under her red blanket were sparkly pink tennis shoes. Immediately, I felt responsible… We didn't get here in time!

I felt a huge surge of guilt that could have consumed me, but at that moment, one of the doors in the overflow opened and Xander came running into the theater with a panicked expression on his face.

Lynnelle ran in behind him and grabbed his arm. "Xander, you can't be in here!" she shouted, pulling on him.

Breaking free of her grasp, he hollered, "Let go of me! Don't touch me! I gotta find my brother!"

I waved my arms, so he could see me. "Xander! Get out of here. This is a triage set-up – only EMTs and a couple of us can be here. You'll just be in the way!"

He looked right at me but I could swear he didn't know who I was. Shoving Lynnelle away each time she tried to block him from entering the theater, he looked around frantically, obviously searching for something or *someone* specific. Suddenly, he saw what he was looking for… a body still mostly covered in rubble. It was a casualty of the dino hybrid attack that was under such a lot of debris that it had so far gone undiscovered by the First Responders.

He ran over and began grabbing and tossing pieces of concrete, metal, wood and ceiling tiles to uncover the buried kid.

"Xander! Are you OK!?!" he shouted. "Oh, Xander, *please* be all right…!

Xander? Does he know another kid with his same name? I wondered. *It's not that common…*

I sprinted over to Xander and knelt down to help him uncover the buried kid. When he removed a large piece of ceiling tile from the kid's face, I was looking at…. XANDER! I looked from the buried Xander to the Xander digging him out. They were almost identical!

"What the heck?" I said, since I could think of nothing else to say at that moment. "Xander?" I said in confusion, placing my hand on the digger's shoulder.

He hit my hand off his shoulder. "I'm not Xander," he said angrily. "*He* is my brother Xander and he's unconscious. He's been under this pile for TOO LONG!"

"Wait — You're Xander's *brother?*" I asked, completely surprised.

"Yeah, we're twins… *obviously.* Name's Sebastian." He turned to me and growled, "Now are you just going to sit there or will you help me free him?"

"Oh, I'm sorry," I said, getting up to go around to the other side of the rubble pile. "Xander said he had a brother, but I didn't know he was a twin," I said, apologetically, grabbing the biggest piece of rubble.

"On three," he said.

I nodded my head. "1… 2… 3… LIFT!" he shouted. We pulled up on the piece but it wouldn't budge — much too heavy.

"No.. no-no-no-no!" Sebastian screamed. "We have to get him out!"

I looked at Xander's unconscious face, and I could tell he didn't have much life left in him. There was probably not enough time to get EMTs over here. And they probably couldn't lift the heavy piece of masonry off Xander, either. I had to do something.

"Stand back!" I ordered Sebastian, giving him a not-so-gentle shove. His first reaction was to shove me back, but when he saw the stern look on my face, he backed up.

I took deep breath and morphed into my *Regem Insuperabilus* to 50 percent, which was big enough for the job at hand. I bent down and bit the huge piece of rubble in two, then knocked the pieces off Xander. Once he was free of debris, I picked him up carefully and placed him on a clear part of the stage floor. Quickly, I de-morphed and knelt next to Xander. I felt his pulse, which was very faint.

Sebastian came closer. "What can we do?" he asked. All his anger was gone. He was just a kid worried for his brother.

"Sebastian, pull down that side curtain. We'll wrap Xander in it so my scales won't hurt him." I directed him.

"Your scales? WHAT?" he shrieked.

"I can get him to the hospital faster than any of the ambulances," I said. "Just get the curtain!"

From the other side of the stage, Lynnelle ran to help Sebastian with the curtain. Together they carefully wrapped the unconscious Xander. I morphed to ten percent, which was just perfect for Sebastian and Lynnelle to lift Xander up and place him on my back. Lynnelle reached over and detached the cord from the stage curtain and looped it around Xander and between two of my protruding scales.

"Go ahead," she shouted. "I got it ready to tighten as you morph," she said, stepping back.

"Sounds good," I said. "Sebastian, climb on Matthew and follow us to the hospital," I said, as I walked carefully around piles of rubble and out to the parking lot where I could morph to 75%. As Matthew morphed, Sebastian crawled up his tail and held on for dear life as Matthew took off at a run behind me.

As we tore away from the school, we could hear Lynnelle's voice on the wind: "GO, GO, GO! Try to break a land-speed record!"

Chapter 27

After we left Centennial High, I looked back over my shoulder every block or so to check on the unconscious Xander as I ran at top speed to the hospital. When we arrived outside Emergency, I de-morphed slowly so the hospital staffers could loosen the cord around Xander before preparing to lift him onto a gurney.

Just then Matthew slid into the parking lot. Sebastian leaped to the ground even before Matthew's de-morphing would have made it an easier jump. He raced over to me and helped the orderlies take his brother off my back. My de-morphing complete, I reached out and hit the DOOR OPEN button, and we all dashed through the double doors.

A young intern met us at the doorway, took in Xander's dire condition in a nano-second and signaled the intake nurse to call for assistance. She immediately pressed an intercom button and called, "STAFF RESPONSE NEEDED IN EMERGENCY!"

In seconds, three nurses came running around the corner. When they spotted us, one nurse assessed the situation instantly and instructed the desk nurse to put out a "CODE 3" as she led us into a treatment cubicle and instructed Sebastian to "step back" from the gurney. She gave him a little shove when he hesitated. The other two nurses began assembling IV stands and monitors that would be needed when the doctors got there.

Within a minute or two, the first nurse had put an oxygen mask on Xander's face and a blood pressure cuff to his left arm and the second nurse was moving a stethoscope around to points on his chest. The third nurse took his temperature with a forehead thermometer, then placed two fingers under his jaw as she looked at her watch and counted the pulse beats. When she nodded her head, I took it as a good sign.

Then the elevator doors opened and two doctors emerged. They strode over to Xander's cubicle, stepped inside, gesturing us to move back even farther. They pulled the curtain closed with a "swish," closing us outside.

Sebastian looked at me and anger flared in his eyes. He reached out and opened the curtain with an even harder "swish" and stepped inside, his hands clenched into fists.

The gray-haired male doctor turned toward Sebastian with a stern look. "Kid, you can't come in here," he said firmly. "Go to the waiting room. Someone will let you know what is happening."

"He's my brother!" Sebastian shouted, trying to step farther into the cubicle.

The first nurse stepped between the doctor and Sebastian. "I'm sorry. We still cannot let you in here," she said softly. "I promise I will personally come to the waiting room and let you know what's going on every step of the way."

That seemed to calm Sebastian down a little. He took a step backward, then hesitated.

He looked at me. "Daniel, I need to be with my brother. I need to know he's ok," he said, and angry tears began snaking down both cheeks.

"Sebastian, I understand that, but the doctors and nurses have to do their work to help him without worrying about any of us," I said, looking him steadily in the eye. "I think you need to call your family to let them know what happened. The news people were outside the high school, remember, so it's anyone's guess what people might have heard by now. And I didn't see Xander's phone on him, so your relatives might have been trying to call him..."

He stared at me with his mouth a little open, then nodded his head in understanding.

The desk nurse came over then, smiling kindly. "The waiting room is right around the corner," she said, pointing the way. "We'll send out Dr. Lingard to keep you kids posted on your friend's situation," she said, and she went back to her seat behind the desk.

Dr. Lingard??! I thought, shaking my head in shock. I headed for the waiting room, that familiar name still ringing in my ears. *Dr. Lingard! I haven't seen him in a year. What good luck for Xander that he's on shift today,* I thought.

When we got to the waiting room, Matthew and I sat down and started talking about the dino hybrid incident while Sebastian paced back and forth, talking on his holo.

"That was a gigantic dinosaur, wasn't it?" Matthew said, sounding a little shaky. "And *two* of them!"

I nodded my head, "Yeah, those two were things I've never seen before," I said. "Too bad we couldn't prevent those nine kids..."

"What nine kids?" he asked with a puzzled look.

"The nine who lost their lives. If we had gotten there sooner..."

"Kids DIED?" Matthew cried, and tears formed in his eyes.

I nodded sadly.

"Do you think it was... y'know?" he asked, carefully avoiding the "J-word" that was thrown around a lot last year.

I shook my head. "No way of knowing about that. Of course, there is no question that it is a hybrid created by *somebody*," I said with complete conviction. "We'll know more when Dad analyzes the samples that Johnny took from the two dead dinos. Andy and Timeer flew the samples to the lab in record time."

I looked over at Sebastian as he hung up his holo. He sighed, then walked over to the seat to my left and sat down.

"My Dad is on his way. He'll be here soon."

I nodded my head, but then remembered about his mom. "Hey, Sebastian, Xander told me about your mother. I'm sorry," I said.

Sebastian looked me, somewhat surprised. "Thanks," he said, mechanically. Then he looked up with a curious expression.

"When did he tell you about our mom? He usually doesn't tell people what happened."

"Well, I think he just needed to stop feeling scared all the time," I said. "He came to Team Triassic Headquarters to see if we could help him. Don't you know that he's been learning martial arts and self-defense with us?" I asked.

He brushed his hand through his hair, remembering something. He looked up, knitting his brows. "Did he have a problem with your training?" he asked. "I thought he quit or something. All I remember is that one night he was crying in his bed after he woke up from a nightmare screaming, 'NO! Andy, NO!'"

Right then and there, I explained to Sebastian the whole unfortunate "training" episode with Andy, Matthew and Xander, including the fact that Xander had previously been wanting to become part of Team Triassic but that the "Scenting Trial" seemed to ruin everything. I told Sebastian that I had been so angry and disappointed at Andy that I was ready to throw my own brother off the Team.

"Andy's your *brother?*" Sebastian asked in amazement.

"Yes, he is. He's a multi-species dino hybrid like me, but his hybrid is *Avian Sinustrodon*, a flying dino with a super sense of smell. That's why he was seeking Xander."

Sebastian looked bewildered. "So… Is Xander part of Team Triassic? Is your brother still on the Team?"

I could understand his confusion, so I hurried to explain about the success of the Monday meeting in my office and how happy I have been ever since, with both my brother back on-board and Xander working to learn the ropes from Kayla and Juli in the Control Room.

"We've been working around his school schedule," I explained, pointing out that our Team Triassic members have a special arrangement with Clark County Schools for online school at Headquarters so we can train for incidents like the one we just experienced.

"Wow!" he said, breathing out deeply and long. "I had no idea! My little brother…"

"Your *little* brother?" I asked, with a tilt of my head. "I thought you were twins."

"Oh, we are," he said, with a little chuckle. "But I'm four minutes older!"

We both laughed then and Matthew joined in, although it didn't seem that his heart was in it. Still, I was happy that the tension in the room was relieved… at least a little.

"So…" Sebastian asked, with upraised eyebrows, "Are there any openings on your Team… like for a guy who is related to one of your newest Team members but is OLDER than he is?" He winked.

I gave a small laugh. "We do have a few openings, actually," I said. "But there is an application procedure…"

"All right, whatever it takes. I'm going to apply for the Team," he said with conviction.

I was just about to tell Sebastian how to contact Juli when the waiting room door flew open and a familiar voice boomed, "Well, there's a happy sight!"

I quickly turned my head, taking in the familiar figure in a white jacket, his glasses low on his nose.

I jumped up, shouting, "Dr. Lingard!" and ran over to wrap my arms around him in a big hug.

Hugging me back, he said, "It's always great for me to see my old patients doing well."

I pulled back from the hug and he looked at me. "Wow, you're looking really great," he said. "Nevertheless, I think you might have need of my services once again… but not for you personally this time, right?"

Sebastian walked up to us then, and I put my arm around his back. "Sebastian, this is Dr. Lingard. He saved my life. I wouldn't be here without him," I said, looking then at the doctor. "Dr. Lingard, it's Sebastian's brother who needs your help the most today."

Dr. Lingard shook Sebastian's hand, saying, "Oh, you're Sebastian? You're the young man I have come to see then."

"Y- Yeah, I'm Sebastian…. My Dad's on his way. Is my brother going to be OK?"

Dr. Lingard smiled kindly. "Your brother has suffered a number of serious injuries, but I am confident that we can restore him to good health," he said. "He's being prepped for surgery at the moment. We can repair his six broken ribs and the tear in his lower intestine and stop the internal bleeding over the next few hours, so you will need to be patient. Are your parents coming?" he asked.

"My mom can't come," he said, matter-of-factly. "She's been a patient in the Psychiatric Annex for a long time. But Dad is on his way."

"Sorry about your mom," Dr. Lingard said. "What's her name? Maybe I know her."

"Her name is Maria... Maria Montgomery."

The doctor thought a moment. "Who's her doctor?" he asked. " Maybe I can look in on her."

"It's Dr. Esterbrook. Do you know her?" Sebastian asked.

"Oh yes!" Dr. Lingard said. "She is very good. We often consult together. After we get your brother fixed up, I'll check in with Dr. Esterbrook about your mom, OK?"

The desk nurse poked her head in the door and handed a note to Dr. Lingard. He read it quickly then looked up at us.

"Your friend Aurora is just down the hall in room 113. She only had to get stitches in her head and her shoulder was dislocated. We're keeping her overnight just to monitor things. Tucker is already in surgery, and we hope for a good result with him. I need to join his surgical team now, so I'll catch up with you later. Oh, by the way, Tucker'll be in recovery for a while, but eventually we plan to have him share a room with Xander on the surgery floor, the 500 rooms, right down the hall from your friend Nick."

"All right, thanks, Dr. Lingard. I'm going up to see Nick now," I said, shaking his hand.

"All right, Daniel. I'll see you around then. Good to meet you," he said to Sebastian, walking out the door and heading towards the elevator.

I started walking towards the elevators, but I quickly turned around to see Matthew heading toward the exit door. *Strange,* I thought. *He didn't say he was leaving.*

Sebastian was still standing just inside the waiting room door, looking unsure of what to do next. I walked back to him.

"Sebastian, why don't you come with me?" I suggested. "You can kill some time."

He nodded his head. We got Nick's room number from the desk nurse and let her know that's where we'd be so she could call us when Mr. Montgomery got there. Then we rode the elevator to the fifth floor and headed for room 524.

I knocked on the door.

When Nick's voice said "Come in," I opened the door and the two of us walked in.

Nick was propped up in bed, attached to an IV on his right arm and a blood pressure monitor on his left. His neck was heavily bandaged and the left side of his head was shaved, but otherwise, he looked pretty good. Angel was leaning up against the wall next to the window, engrossed in something on his holo. He looked up, saluted at me, and went back to his holo.

"Oh, hey guys," Nick said. "Thanks for coming. I need to get filled in... My Elliott wrist holo seems to have gone missing..."

"There's plenty of time for that, Nick," I said, pulling a chair up next to his bed. "First, how are you feeling?" Sebastian pulled a chair up next to me.

"It doesn't hurt. It just feels numb," he replied. "Hi, Xander."

I shook my head no and laughed. "Nick, this is Sebastian, Xander's twin brother," I explained.

I guess Angel wasn't all that engrossed, because he looked up and cried, "What? No way!"

Sebastian laughed. "Yeah, I'm Xander's twin brother. He's here in the hospital," he said.

Nick tilted his head a little. "What do you mean 'He's here'?" he asked.

Sebastian and I looked at each other, both realizing that Nick and Angel were *really* out of the loop.

"Xander is one of the kids seriously injured by the dino," I said. "He is in surgery as we speak," I told them.

Nick sat up. "Are you serious!?!" he cried.

Sebastian and I both nodded our heads.

Nick looked down. "Poor kid! He's been through so much," he said sadly.

"I know," I said, "but we have to have hope. Dr. Lingard is part of the surgical team, so Xander has the best chance..."

Nick and Angel both nodded their heads.

"So how long are you going to be here?" I asked Nick.

"The nurse said I'll be out of here in a couple of hours, when my Dad gets here. At first, they thought I'd have to stay overnight, but now I won't. The nurse said she's coming right back with another IV bag to replace my fluids. When it's done, I can be discharged," he said, pointing at the IV bag that was nearly empty. "I guess I bled quite a lot."

"You bet," I said, reaching over into the open wardrobe and pulling out a blood-stained sweatshirt. "I'd say your favorite concert shirt has bit the dust." Nick nodded sadly and I dropped the shirt into the wastebasket.

Angel put away his holo, plainly now in a mood to join our conversation. He pulled out of his zippered sweatshirt, smoothing out the t-shirt underneath, and tossed the sweatshirt to his brother.

"So... Daniel... Do you know where that dino came from... who made it... what it's made of?" Nick asked.

I shook my head. "No," I said. "Andy and Timeer should be back at

Dad's lab by now with some blood and tissue samples that Johnny took. Dad will get to work on them right away."

Hearing a light knock on the door, we all turned to see a nurse carrying an IV bag walking in, followed by a girl with red hair who had on a nurse's aide uniform and was carrying a clipboard. The nurse went to the IV stand, replaced the IV bag without a word and left the room.

Referring to her clipboard, the nurse's aide said, "Hello, Nick." Then, looking up and seeing all of us, she said, "Oh, I didn't realize you had company. Hi everyone! My name is Evelyn. I'm a volunteer here at this hospital."

When her gaze fell on me, her eyes and mouth all opened wide "Oh, my gosh!" she cried, instinctively covering her wide-open mouth with the top of the clipboard. "You're Daniel! Daniel of Team Triassic!" She reached out her hand. "It's an honor to meet you!"

"It's nice to meet you too, Evelyn," I said, shaking her hand warmly. "And thanks for helping to treat Nick."

She laughed. "No gratitude needed. I'm just a nurse's aide… no treatment at these hands," she said. "The person in charge of Nick's care is my Dad."

"Your Dad?" I asked, puzzled.

"Yep," she said. "I think you may know him. My name is Evelyn Lingard. Name sound familiar?" she asked with a wink, ducking her head with the clipboard across the end of her nose. I had seen that same expression often last year… If the loops on the metal top of her clipboard was instead a pair of reading glasses, I could be looking at a younger version of Dr. Lingard!

"OMG!" I said.

Chapter 30

Nick, Angel, and I shook our heads and dropped our mouths open in shock.

"Really!?" Nick exclaimed, leaning forward in his bed.

Evelyn laughed again and looked at each of us individually as she said, "Yes… Dr. Lingard… is my Dad."

Still amazed, none of us said a word.

Evelyn turned her attention to me then. "He talked about you the most," she said, wagging her pointer finger at me.

"Really? I- I didn't know. I was just one of his patients, after all," I said.

"Yeah, he talked about you a lot last year. Then he stopped mentioning you," she said, and a puzzled look crossed her face.

"I guess it was because I wasn't here anymore," I said. "He had other patients to concentrate on."

"Your Dad's a hero," Nick said.

She turned and faced him. "I'm sure he is," she said, sighing deeply. She tucked her clipboard under her arm and went out the door with a little wave.

What did she mean by that? I wondered.

Any further thought became impossible as Elliott's alert was suddenly coming through on the wrist-holos Angel and I were wearing and another one on the shelf of the wardrobe.

"UPDATE FOR TEAM TRIASSIC!" Elliott announced sternly.

"CENTENNIAL HOSPITAL'S ER IS OVERLOADED AND DR. LINGARD ASKED FOR DANIEL TO RETURN TO COMFORT INCOMING PATIENTS UNTIL DOCTORS CAN TREAT THEM. DANIEL, YOU'LL NEED TO STOP BY THE DESK AND GET A MASK AND GLOVES. SEBASTIAN, YOUR DAD HAS ARRIVED. MEET HIM IN THE FIRST FLOOR WAITING ROOM."

The holo-feed paused, then Elliott was back, his tone uncharacteristically kindhearted. "NICK, I AM RELIEVED THAT YOUR INJURY WAS NOT MORE SERIOUS. YOU WILL BE DISCHARGED AT 4:45 PM. MEET YOUR DAD AT THE SOUTH ENTRANCE PROMPTLY AT 5 PM FOR A RIDE HOME." And he was gone.

"That Elliott never stops amazing me," I said, as I gave Nick a quick hug goodbye and followed Sebastian out the door.

"See you tomorrow," I called over my shoulder.

When we emerged from the elevator in ER, chaos was all around us. Every cubicle was filled, some with patients undergoing treatment and others with kids awaiting their turn. Sebastian went into the waiting room to meet his father. When the desk nurse caught sight of me, she held up a mask and a pair of latex gloves. I made my way through the maze of kids on gurneys, their parents and other adults and orderlies. I took the mask and gloves with a quick "Thanks" to the nurse.

I threaded through the crowd again to the first cubicle with a kid awaiting treatment. When I poked my head through the curtain, a blond-haired boy of about fourteen looked over at me, quickly wiping away the tears that covered his face.

"Hi," I said. "I'm Daniel. Can I stay with you for a while… until the doctor comes?"

He sniffed, then reached up gingerly and wiped his runny nose with his sleeve, a motion that obviously hurt. He winced, then "remembered his manners" and said quietly, "OK. I'm William."

"William, do you know what your injuries are?" I asked.

I could hardly hear him, so I leaned closer. His voice was young but sounded…somehow *sophisticated*.

"I heard the nurse say 'broken ribs' and I can tell my left arm and left leg are broken – a huge piece of cement landed on me after the dino threw me against the wall – and my head hurts really bad…" Tears flooded out of his eyes, but this time he just let them flow.

I reached out to pat his right arm lightly. "This has been a horrible day for you and for lots of others," I said. "But I know you will be brave as the doctors fix you up. Are your parents coming?"

"My dad is out of town on business, but he's coming tonight. Mom is on her way from Henderson," he said, adding, "I'm glad someone can stay with me. It's so scary to be here alone."

At that moment, the curtain swished open and an intern and two nurses strode in, the one nurse pushing an IV stand.

The doctor looked at me and asked, "Are you family?"

Before I could answer, he told me, "Go wait in the waiting room."

Following his no-nonsense orders, I waved at William and left the cubicle, as the one nurse was hooking William up to the two bags on the IV stand while the other one was beginning to cut away his clothes. The doctor was moving a stethoscope around his upper chest.

I looked around for a few minutes, trying to decide where I could be of some help – without getting in the way of medical personnel – when a nurse emerged from a cubicle and I caught sight of a familiar face on the gurney inside. I pretended to "knock" on the curtain and poked my head in the cubicle.

"Daniel!" Aurora cried. "Come in! Hey, it's good to see you again," she said with a big smile.

"How are you feeling?" I asked.

She moved her hand to her forehead and gently touched the bandage over that big gash. "I'm better. The doctors had to pop my shoulder back in place – NOT something I would recommend, since it hurt like… you-know-what — and, as you can see, they stitched me up. Fourteen stitches!" she said, wincing. "Still, I'm one of the lucky ones, I know."

"Right. I understand that nine kids didn't make it," I said, sadly.

"NINE?!" she exclaimed. "Have you heard any names yet? I'm so afraid that my best friend Annie might be one of them. We had both been tossed against the wall by the dino, but she pushed me away when the ceiling came down and I couldn't see anything but her sparkly pink shoes after that."

A feeling of dread seized me, as I remembered what I saw in the temporary morgue earlier. I tried to cover myself by saying, as casually as possible, "Let me check." I stepped outside the curtain to speak quietly into my wrist-holo. "Elliott, do we have names of the deceased yet?"

Elliott responded immediately, copying my quiet tone, but he was reluctant to answer my question.

I excused myself from Aurora's cubicle and walked into an empty section of hallway. "Elliott, I am alone. Just tell me... Were any of the nine killed named Annie?"

"AN ANNIE FLYNN IS ON THE LIST FROM THE MORGUE DID YOU KNOW HER, DANIEL?"

"No," I told him, "but she's the friend of a friend."

"MY SINCERE CONDOLENCES," Elliott intoned and he clicked off.

When I returned to Aurora's cubicle, she could tell from the look on my face that the news was not good. "Is Annie's last name 'Flynn'?" I asked.

"Y-y-ess," she said, worry filling her face.

"I'm sorry," I said, moving to place my hand on her back and rub it gently. "I don't think she suffered... and she's in a better place."

Aurora nodded her head. "She saved me," she said. "My arm is dislocated because Annie pushed me... hard. I looked back, and big pieces of the ceiling were piled right where she had been." She broke down in sobs.

I kept patting her back, not knowing what else to do. Trying to think of comforting words, I said, "Hey, she's looking down at you with a smile on her face. She saved you because she cared so much about you," I said. "Your friend Annie is a hero."

She nodded her head. "I know, but I miss her so much already. But thank you, Daniel, for telling me and for being here with me. You have such a kind heart," she said, reaching out just a little to touch my hand.

I don't know why, but it occurred to me right then that maybe Team Triassic could offer Aurora a diversion to help her grieve her friend. I remembered how our martial arts and self-defense training helped Xander with his lingering trauma. Maybe it might help Aurora.

"Well... Here's something for you to talk over with your parents sometime," I began slowly. "You probably don't know that Team Triassic has been offering classes in martial arts and self-defense, and we've talked about adding some other classes. If you think you might want to try out a session or two, it would give you the opportunity to get to know our Team. They're really top-notch kids..."

I would have gone on (and on and on, probably), but Aurora sat straight up in bed and said, "YES! YES! YES!" with so much enthusiasm that I almost forgot she had just been through an unbelievable trauma.

"Team Triassic has been my dream ever since that celebration at Molasky Stadium!" she gushed. "When I saw that Kayla and Lynnelle were female dino hybrids on the Team, I started thinking you might consider adding a female *Triceratops* hybrid... even though I have never actually tried out any of my hybrid traits. I was thinking that maybe someday..."

"Well, today just might be 'someday,'" I said with a grin. "As soon as you are healed, come see me at Headquarters... if your parents say ok..."

"Did we hear the word 'parents'?" a man's voice said outside the cubicle. The curtain swished aside and a man and woman who were obviously Aurora's mom and dad rushed in. I stepped back so they could smother their daughter with love. After a few minutes of mumbled "I wish I could have been here sooner," "I love you's" and other endearments, they stood up, noticing me for the first time. Mr. and Mrs. Brewer and I introduced ourselves and spent a couple of minutes in small-talk; then I left them alone with their daughter.

I'm sure that I'll be seeing more of Aurora, I thought to myself as I walked over to the waiting room to see what Sebastian was up to.

Chapter 31

I was about five feet in front of the door to the waiting room when the door suddenly flew open. A tall man in a leather jacket and baggy jeans burst through the doorway and shoved me aside roughly.

"Out of my way, kid!" he ordered.

Then Sebastian was through the doorway, chasing after the big guy.

"Dad, stop!" he shouted, running to position himself in front of the man, trying to block him from moving forward. Putting both hands against his dad's chest, he spoke firmly. "They won't let us see him!"

The man shoved Sebastian aside and strode over to the desk. Sebastian and I followed, but there was little we could do.

The man I figured was Mr. Montgomery was shouting at the desk nurse, "Look lady, I don't give a damn about what you say! I want to see my son!"

He pounded on the desk so hard that the nurse's computer monitor jumped. He reached over the high desk and grabbed the room list, ran his finger down to find the name he wanted, then flung it back at the nurse, who ducked just in time to avoid getting hit in the head.

Turning on his heel, the out-of-control Mr. Montgomery shoved his way through the startled crowd, heading around the corner toward the elevators.

There is NO WAY I'm letting this man anywhere near Xander, I decided. I ran to catch up, passed him and turned around to face him, planting my feet firmly. I held my arms out, hands in a "Stop" position.

"Get out of my way!" he snarled, pushing hard against my unyielding hands.

Planting my feet even more firmly, I leaned toward him.

"NO!" I said back with "attitude." I did not move a muscle.

He cracked his knuckles and shuffled from one foot to the other with a swagger.

"Boy, I am not going to tell you again," he said, threateningly. He leaned all his weight against my hands. I didn't move.

I leaned closer and got up in his face.

"Then go ahead and knock me out of your way. That'll be the last thing you'll remember for a while!" I said, as my eyes turned red and my body prepared itself for a battle.

He put his hand on my chest, ready to shove me. Then suddenly, out of the corner of my eye, I saw Sebastian jump up against the wall and do a 90-degree kick, nailing his dad in the side of the head. I stood there, stunned, as Xander's "older brother" did a little spin in the air and landed on his feet, facing his father in a fighting position.

"Get away from Daniel!" Sebastian barked, just as his dad keeled over backward.

Mr. Montgomery lay on the ground for a few seconds, dazed, then propped himself up on an elbow. "Ooohh, what hit me?" he asked, holding the side of his head. He looked up at Sebastian, then at me, then back to Sebastian.

"Did you just KICK me?" he asked, dumbfounded.

"I did," Sebastian said with quite a little "attitude." His arms were crossed and his facial expression grim.

"How DARE you?" his dad said, getting up, brushing off his jacket and adjusting his sagging waistband.

Before he had a chance to say anything else, Sebastian leaned right into his dad's face and spoke through clenched teeth. "You have no right to disregard the rules in this hospital OR push people around," he said firmly. "Xander is in bad condition. I saw it myself. He's barely alive. And this kid right here…" — he pointed at me — "He made it his Number-One priority to get him to the hospital *fast*. AND THIS IS HOW YOU REPAY HIM! BY DISREPECTING HIM! Maybe you think he should've just left Xander back there to die!" Sebastian turned his back on his dad and leaned his forehead against the wall.

I took a step towards Sebastian, very much aware that this family dispute had drawn the attention of the crowded ER. Quite a few people had been drawn to the elevator lobby by the commotion. They stood there, looking at us out of the corner of their eyes and whispering among themselves, shaking their heads.

"Come on, guys…" I began.

Sebastian cut me off. "Stay out of this, Daniel. This man here needs to hear this and he needs to hear it NOW." He stood close to his dad and spoke in low, measured tones.

"You never cared about us. For *years*. Xander went to these guys for help when he never could get over feeling scared after what happened with Mom. You didn't know this, because Xander could never tell you how scared he was. All we ever hear from you is that we have to 'Be tough,' that we're supposed to be your 'soldiers' and take orders and constant criticism from you. You've never been the sort of father any kid deserves. Now Xander might die, so I am going to keep you from hurting him anymore. You will get into my brother's room over my dead body!" He took up a stance in front of the elevator and wiped his face with the back of his hand.

His father stared at him for a few brief moments, stunned. "Oh, Sebastian, I'm-" but Sebastian cut him off by holding up his hand in front of his face.

"Save it! I don't want you talking to me for a while… maybe forever," he said angrily.

A lady in the crowd applauded softly and mouthed, "Good going, kid!" to Sebastian. Mr. Montgomery stood stock-still for a minute, then did an almost military about-face and headed for the exit. Strangers he passed showed their feelings by stepping in his way or making comments to him under their breath. A collective sigh of relief seemed to spread through the ER after he was outside.

Sebastian and I got into the elevator and rode up to the surgical floor. We walked a little way down the hall, where there was a long bench outside the operating theater and we sat down. When Sebastian placed his head in his hands, I put my arm over his shoulders.

He began crying. "I'm sorry," he said.

I shook my head. "For what? For saying what needed to be said? At least you got it off your chest," I told him.

He nodded his head. "I know, but I wish it didn't happen here in the hospital and I wish you didn't see it. What will you and the Team think of us now?" He put both hands in front of his face as he sobbed. I tried to comfort him with pats on his back, but he just kept crying.

Dr. Lingard came around the corner and saw us.

"Oh, guys, what's going on here?" he asked.

Sebastian and I looked up at him. Sebastian hurriedly wiped tears off his face with both hands.

I knew I was the one to say something. "Some stuff just went down between Sebastian and his father," I said.

Sebastian nodded his head at him. Dr. Lingard nodded his head once – his "I get it" gesture — and sat down next to Sebastian and patted his back.

"It's all right. Situations like the one today with your brother are hard for everyone," he said. "And you have the added tragedy with your mom, too. Your family has been through a lot," he said, kindly.

"I'm just tired of the way he's been treating me and Xander," Sebastian said.

Dr. Lingard tilted his head and scratched the back of his head.

"What do you mean? Has he been mistreating you and your brother?" he asked.

"No, he's not physically abusive – not anymore, anyway – but he demands absolute obedience and he's so paranoid. We can't even have our friends over without him interrogating them or us. He always says that people want to get into our house because they have 'ulterior motives' – whatever that means! It sucks," he said, shaking his head sadly.

"That sounds terrible," Dr. Lingard said.

"Yeah," I agreed. "I had no idea..."

We sat in silence for a few seconds. Then Dr. Lingard sat up straight, clapped one and rose. "I did come to give you some news, boys. Want to hear it?"

I wasn't sure that I wanted to hear what he had to say. After all, he had just come out of the operating room and his scrubs were just a little bloody. But he had a positive look on his face, so I decided to be ready for the "news."

"Good news?" I asked, ducking my head down a little.

"I'd say so," Dr. Lingard said, smiling. "I came to tell you two that Xander is out of surgery and every indication is that he's going to be ok."

Sebastian stood up and faced the doctor, sighing in relief. He breathed, "Oh my god! Really!?"

Dr. Lingard nodded his head. "Yep. He's in Recovery. We'll let you two know when you can see him." He adjusted his scrubs a bit to cover up most of the blood spots, then took off his surgical gloves to shake our hands.

"Thank you so much, Dr. Lingard, for everything you've done. Not just for Xander, but for me too," I said, shaking his hand warmly.

"Yeah, Dr. Lingard, really, thanks," Sebastian said, shaking hands.

"Hey now, no need to thank me. It's my job to help people," the doctor said.

"I know, but I just really feel like I can't say thanks to you enough," I said.

He smiled and began to turn away, then stopped. "I *was* wondering, though… Was the dinosaur attacking today the same as the one that almost got you last year? A SpinoRex, if I remember correctly?"

"No, it definitely was not," I told him. "And there were *two* of them – looked kind of like twins, actually – but for some bizarre reason, the one dino fought with the other one and killed it before they got near Centennial. I just cannot imagine what a massacre today would have been if both of those beasts made a coordinated attack!"

"So you have no idea what kind of monsters they were?" Dr. Lingard asked.

I smiled a little. "Well, not yet," I said, 'but we will… I had the guys get equipment from Dad's lab and go take blood and tissue samples from both of the dinosaur carcasses. When Dad analyzes the samples, he should be able to identify the complete DNA profile of both animals."

"That's wonderful!" the doctor said, stopping a few seconds again to think. "You know, I miss your Dad, Daniel. Last year he and I got to talk at least a few times a week – when you were snoozing away, that is – but we've kind of lost touch. I missed the Open House, so I've never seen his new lab. And I'm really interested in his dino hybrid research. Do you think he'd mind if I stopped in sometime… when he has free time, of course?"

"Dr. Lingard, I am positive he'd love it! We talk about you at dinner all the time. Here's his holo call number." I tapped it into my phone and it popped up instantly on the doctor's phone. "I'll let him know you'll be calling."

"Thanks, Daniel. Gotta run. Keep up the good work. Everybody is counting on all of you!"

He gave me a fatherly pat on the shoulder and turned back toward the operating theater.

"Tell Xander I said hi," he called over his shoulder as he rounded the corner. "I'm going to check with the surgical team treating your friend Tucker, too. Catch up with you later!" And he was gone.

Sebastian and I wandered down the hall and stopped at the closest Nurses Station to learn if Xander's room was assigned yet.

"Yes, it's all ready for him... room 519A," a young nurse-in-training told us with a dazzling smile.

Room 519 was a two-bed semi-private room way down the hallway, but I was happy to see that it was pretty close to the fifth floor waiting room. *If we can't always be in the room with Xander — and Tucker later, maybe —* I thought, *at least we can be close by.*

I pushed the door slowly, peering around at the large room as it opened. Half of the room to my left was closed off with a curtain. (Awaiting Tucker?) When I walked across the room to look at the view of the valley, my gaze dropped to the parking lot below, where I noticed a familiar-looking figure seated on the curb. It looked like Matthew, and he seemed to be... crying.

I headed back for the door, telling Sebastian over my shoulder, "Give me a few minutes. I'll be right back."

"OK," he said. "I'm hungry... You?" When I nodded, he said, "I'm going to make a snack run to the cafeteria," and he followed me to the elevator.

On the ground floor, Sebastian turned right toward the cafeteria and I went left to the parking lot. Once outside, I didn't try to "sneak up" on Matthew, but he didn't notice me until my shadow cast over him. He jumped up, wiped his face with his sleeve, then wrapped his arms around me, sobbing and trying to catch his breath. I held him close and patted his back.

He sucked in large gulps of breath, trying to talk. After a couple of unsuccessful attempts, he managed to get it out: "Those kids are dead because of that... thing..." he said. "I didn't do enough to stop it! And now I'm sitting here, doing nothing to help. I am such a loser."

I moved back and held my hands on his shoulders. His gaze was on the ground.

"Matthew... please look at me," I said, kindly. When he looked up at me, I told him in all sincerity, "You are <u>not</u> a loser, not in any way. None of this is your fault. All of us did everything we could to stop that monster and save those kids. And we DID save a lot of people. It could've been so much worse, but we stopped the bloodshed. Us. Together," I said.

He nodded his head with his eyes shut and wiped new tears off his face.

"But whose fault *is* it?" he asked, needing an answer.

"Those dino hybrids today were a breakthrough design by *someone*," I explained. "It is that someone who is at fault for all of the deaths, injuries and destruction. Everything that happened at Centennial High School today is exclusively that scientist's fault. We are lucky, however, that the one dino killed the other one before they got to the high school, or things would have been so much worse."

Matthew nodded in agreement, but he still had questions. "Do you know... how many people are dead?" He hesitated. "Besides the one I-I... the one I know about, I mean..." he said, and another tear ran down his cheek.

"The number I heard was nine killed. I know the name of only one, though, but Elliott wants her name kept confidential until her family knows," I said. Putting my hand on his back, I said, "Come on with me. We can wait for Xander in his room. Special permission from the floor nurse!" I added with a wink, hoping to lighten Matthew's sadness a bit.

"OK," he said softly. We walked together to the elevator and rode up to 5.

When he followed me into the room and caught sight of Sebastian on the window sill, Matthew jumped in shock and looked like he might keel over. Following his line of sight, I knew to grab him around his back to steady him and explain.

"No, this isn't Xander, although I can see why you'd think it is. Xander is still in Recovery. This is his brother Sebastian," I told Matthew.

"His OLDER brother, the one with the great hair," Sebastian said, releasing his ponytail with a toss of his head that let loose his longer hair. He smiled and reached out to shake Matthew's still-trembling hand.

"Gosh," Matthew said, "you guys almost gave me a heart attack!" He walked over to a chair and plopped down. When Sebastian hesitated to take the remaining chair, looking at me, I made a grand sweeping gesture to show the chair was his. As he settled into the comfy seat, I sat down on the wide window sill, sliding aside a delicious-looking assortment of snacks that he must have bought for us.

Everybody was silent for a few minutes. Then Matthew's long sighs made it clear to Sebastian and me that he still had lots on his mind, so I handed some Doritos to Sebastian. He and I munched on snacks while we let our friend talk, mostly adding "Uh-huh" or "You're right" or other responses that let him "get it out." After about five or ten minutes of this mostly one-sided conversation, a tap-tap on the door let us know we had a visitor.

Come in!" Sebastian and I called in unison.

Dr. Lingard stepped through the door, then stopped, as though he had entered the wrong room. With a tilt of his head, he "apologized." "Oh, sorry fellas... I didn't realize this was the Fifth Floor Waiting Room!" As he walked into the room, Sebastian showed his good manners by getting up to give the doctor his seat.

"I just wanted to stop by to fill you in on your friends... and *relatives*," he said, looking at Sebastian. "Xander is still in Recovery, of course – He'll be there for another ninety minutes or so, I'd say; so if you guys want to go down to the cafeteria and get something to eat, now would be a good time."

"Good idea," I said. "I'm starved!" Sebastian nodded, hiding three empty snack wrappers under his leg.

"I'm not hungry," Matthew said, looking down at the floor. It was obvious to me that – even after talking about all of it — he was still wrestling with some serious trauma about what he saw during the dino attack, and he hadn't touched any of the yummy snacks on the window sill.

Dr. Lingard caught on right away and turned his attention to Matthew. He pulled his chair close to him and put his hand on Matthew's shoulder.

"Son, are you OK?" he asked. Matthew just shook his head.

"He's had a very traumatic day," I explained to the doctor. "He saw the body of one of the kids killed at Centennial. And even though we have tried to convince him otherwise, he still feels personally responsible because we couldn't save that kid or others."

Dr. Lingard shook his head sadly, speaking directly to Matthew. "Yes, today's tragedy is nothing like I've ever seen before. It is absolutely expected that this is hard for you to bear. Last year was kind of crazy with the SpinoRex, but even though Daniel *almost* lost his life then, no one did die. And Nick came out of it all with just some cuts and bruises. Today has been a very different scenario."

Matthew broke down again, remembering.

Dr. Lingard moved to sit closer to him. "Young man," he said, kindly, "you have experienced something that no young person — *or anyone* — should experience; and it will take time for you to come to terms with it. I think the best thing for you to do now is to go home. I'm sure your parents are worried about you. You need to be with them now."

Matthew nodded, and I could tell that the doctor's words had gotten through to him. He wiped tears away and took a deep breath.

"Thank you, doctor. I appreciate you trying to help me," he said, looking down.

Dr. Lingard reached over and brought Matthew's head up to face him. He put his hands on Matthew's shoulders and said, "You can always talk to me, Matthew. I'm here to listen." He handed Matthew his personal business card and stood up, gesturing to me to follow him out of the room.

Out in the hall, Dr. Lingard walked on for a few feet and turned to face me.

"Look, Daniel," he said, "Matthew is not in a good state of mind. I think he might need some counseling. It's ok for him to go home today, but please keep a close eye on him."

"I agree with you, doctor," I said. "We'll watch out for him. I'll ask Nick's Dad to drive him home. He's coming to pick Nick up at 5," I said. I pulled out my holo and sent Mr. Williamson a request:

DANIEL Can you please take Matthew home when you pick up Nick? He's upset and should not be alone.

Within ten seconds, I got a reply:

WILLIAMSON ESQ Absolutely! And I'll make sure he's with his parents. No simple drop-off!

I sent a thank-you, then turned back to Dr. Lingard, who had been catching up on his messages while I was holo-texting. When he paused and looked up, I took the opportunity to bring up Evelyn.

"So… you didn't tell me you had a daughter," I said. "In all of our talks last year…"

He laughed. "I see, so you met Evelyn?" he asked.

"Yeah, she seems nice," I said.

"Yes, she's a sweetheart. She's around your age," he said.

I nodded. "I figured so. Do you have other kids?" I asked.

He smiled. "I have two teenage daughters and a son, who's almost four. And we have another child coming this year."

My mouth dropped open a little. "Your wife is pregnant?" I asked, with excitement in my voice.

He smiled and nodded his head. "Yep, and I'm hoping it's a boy – so everything in the family is evenly balanced," he said with a grin. "My birthday comes about when she's due. If our baby arrives then, it'll be the best 38th birthday present *ever!*" he said happily.

"Dang," I said. "You don't look a day over 30," I said.

He smiled and patted my shoulder. "You're too kind," he said, just as his holo beeped. "Gotta run!" and he was off down the hall, disappearing around the corner.

I went back into Xander's room, where Matthew and Sebastian were engrossed in the newscast on the wall-mounted TV.

As I walked between Matthew and the TV, he clicked the remote to "Pause" and looked at me with a questioning face.

"So… what was so secret between you and the doctor?" he asked, in a slightly unfriendly tone.

I tried to play it off as nothing much, saying only, "No secret — The doc just suggested that one of us get you home safely today. Nick's Dad is coming to pick him up when he's discharged in a couple of hours, so I asked Mr. Williamson to drive you to your place and he said he'd be glad to. No biggie."

"OK, I guess," Matthew said, clicking the forward arrow on the remote. As the newscast resumed, I turned my back and sent a quick holo-text to Nick:

DANIEL Hey Nick, Matthew is having a hard time. Dr. Lingard and I think he shouldn't walk home alone. Your dad said he'd take him home when he comes to get you. Swing by 519 and pick him up, ok?

NICK Sure, no prob. See you soon!

DANIEL Thanks for being there for him. You should rest, too, so stay home. Catch you tomorrow at Headquarters if you're up to it. Just… make sure Matthew's ok.

NICK Got it.

I walked over to my seat on the window sill and settled in to catch up on local news. Not surprisingly, the lead story was all about the attack on Centennial High. Mark O'Brien, the Action News anchor, assumed a very grim pose as he did the lead-in to the story:

"Early this afternoon – at 12:23 pm exactly – one of two rogue dinosaurs that have been seen around town in recent days attacked the theater wing of Centennial High School, bringing destruction and death to our community. Local officials note that this attack could have been even worse, but the two dinosaurs fought each other prior to the attack… a fight that ended one dinosaur's life. For more on this story, we take you to Chloe Simpson, on location outside the theater wing of Centennial High School. Chloe?"

The camera panned the school parking lot briefly before focusing on a very young female reporter with blonde "anchor hair" and wearing a green jumpsuit.

"Thank you, Mark and hello, Las Vegas, on this sad day. I'm Chloe Simpson of KTNV Action News, on location here at Centennial High, the site of today's horrible tragedy. As you can see by the massive destruction behind me, a rogue dinosaur – probably a manmade hybrid — charged right through the solid stone-and-brick wall into the school's theater, causing devastation to the building, but – more horribly – causing injury and death to students and faculty inside."

She stepped gingerly over low piles of rubble as the camera followed her toward the hole in the building. Three large Metro policemen stepped into her path when she was about fifteen feet away from the broken wall.

Taking their hint, the reporter stopped and turned toward the camera.

"As you can see, our excellent Metro force is on the job to ensure that no one else is injured here today. But we have been told that nine Centennial students have lost their lives and more than twenty others are injured. Some students escaped with minor injuries, but at least five are listed in critical condition at local hospitals.

"Many more deaths and injuries would certainly have happened if not for the Team Triassic Alert System that had full-size dino hybrids on site within minutes. Some other members of Team Triassic escorted many students away from danger, while the Team's dino hybrids fought and killed the beast. Team members also worked with First Responders to tend to the needs of the injured."

The reporter beckoned to her left and a middle-aged woman in a sundress came into the frame.

"This is Mary Gillespie, who lives nearby. Mrs. Gillespie, please tell our viewers what you saw today."

A very nervous Mrs. Gillespie spoke haltingly. "I-I w-was just walking Geoffrey – h-he's our d-dog – and-and-and I saw a h-huge dinosaur-like thing with a kid st-strapped to h-his back… It-it took off r-running so fast! It-it was amazing!"

Chloe smiled into the camera. "Viewers, what Mrs. Gillespie has just described is one way that Team Triassic assisted First Responders who could have become overwhelmed by the enormity of this tragedy. This is how one injured student got to the hospital for emergency treatment – strapped to the back of a fully-morphed dino hybrid!"

Pausing to let the imagined scene settle into viewers' minds, Chloe moved off-camera to allow the cameraman to pan the devastated area. He walked diagonally toward the large hole in the wall, catching a partial view of the huge tarp-covered carcass of the dinosaur splayed out behind three school buses parked to obstruct public view. Before he could get a better shot, a large hand went up in front of his lens and Metro moved him back, where he once again focused on Chloe, who continued her report.

"Earlier today, I had the opportunity to interview one of the young women of Team Triassic, Lynnelle McPherson, who informed me that the creature that attacked Centennial today was probably not a natural-born dinosaur, but rather it *could be* a new dino hybrid that was *created* by someone. Let's hear what Lynnelle had to tell me."

The scene cut to the interview with Lynnelle, who was speaking into Chloe's microphone.

"It was a very scary new type of dino, yes," Lynnelle was saying, "but luckily, thanks to our alert system and Daniel's dino hybrid's great eyesight, we spotted the two beasts headed straight for the school. We all watched in shock on our holos as the two of them fought to the death. This unexpected battle gave Daniel and members our Team the chance to get to Centennial within minutes after the attacking dino broke in. Inside the theater, it was a terrible battle, but we got many of the kids out of danger and Daniel killed the beast. I only wish we could have saved everyone," she said. She looked right into the camera and said, angrily, "I don't know why over the past year, rogue dinos have attacked *schools*. Something is up for sure."

The camera faded back to Chloe on location.

"Hmmm… an interesting perspective from a young Las Vegan and Team Triassic member. Thank you, Lynnelle, for filling us in," she said, looking off-camera, as though Lynnelle was standing there. Turning back, she continued, "As you just heard from Lynnelle McPherson, people around here are giving Team Triassic founder Daniel Robertson lots of the credit for stopping the massacre here at Centennial today. And we have just learned that it was Daniel whom Mrs. Gillespie described as the 'dino-ambulance' that transported a gravely injured teenager to the hospital. We tried looking for Daniel today here at the school, but he's been at the hospital all day helping the people who are injured. What a hero! That's all we have for now. Back to you, Mark."

I was furious! I stood up and turned off the TV, flinging the remote across the room.

Sebastian and Matthew looked at me, stunned by my anger.

"Daniel, what's wrong?" Sebastian asked.

"Yeah, bro, what is it?" Matthew asked

I shook my head angrily. "They made it sound like I deserve all the credit for what happened today. THAT IS NOT THE WAY IT WAS!" I shouted at the black TV screen.

Sebastian and Matthew looked at each other, not knowing what to say. Then Sebastian asked meekly, "Weren't you the first one to spot it?"

"NO! That's the whole point… It was Juli and Kayla back at Headquarters. They'd been monitoring our citywide cameras for a few days, tracking what turned out to be those two dinos. THEY put out the alarm. THEY coordinated all of us. And EVERYBODY PLAYED A PART in destroying that monster before it could do any more damage. A few of us fought the beast, but it was ANGEL, not me, who killed it! WE WORKED TOGETHER. We are a TEAM! Today was NOT a one-man show!"

Sebastian ducked his head, but I could tell he had to say something.

"WHAT?!" I barked at him.

"Well, Daniel, I think you should contact that reporter and get her to set the record straight," he said, evenly. "Why don't you send her a holo?"

I looked at Matthew, who nodded. Right away, I knew the stress of the day had just spilled out of me and landed all over my friends. I felt terrible.

"Sorry, guys. I don't know what got into me," I said. Sebastian walked over and picked up the remote, then put his arm around my shoulders.

"It's ok, Daniel," he said. "We have all had a horrible day. But I think you should holo that reporter... What was her name... Chloe something?"

"You're right. I want people to know the real story. I'll do it tonight," I said. I pulled out my holo and put a Reminder Alert in to Elliott, so I wouldn't get distracted later and forget to set things right with the media.

I was still focused on controlling my anger about the TV thing about a half-hour later when the door opened and an orderly pushed Xander into the room on a gurney. A second orderly followed and the two men grabbed a very limp-looking Xander by his shoulders and legs and swung him gently onto his hospital bed. The first orderly fluffed the pillow around his head and "tucked him in" while the other one pushed the empty gurney into the hallway, returning with an IV stand and bank of monitors that he positioned next to Xander's bed. Neither man acknowledged us or spoke a word to us or each other. The transfer was complete in two minutes and both men walked out and closed the door behind them.

Seeing Xander put all thought of my dispute with the reporter Chloe out of my mind. I had been so afraid that I would never see him again – alive, that is – that a feeling of warm relief washed over me. All three of us approached his bed cautiously, as we couldn't really tell if he was conscious or not. We stood there looking at each other, not knowing what to do next.

Then Xander opened his eyes slowly. He looked from one of us to the other, settling on his brother and smiling weakly.

"Hi," he said softly.

Sebastian leaned over and hugged his head carefully. "Xander, thank God you're all right," he said, struggling not to cry.

"I'm good, I think" Xander said. "What HAPPENED?"

I took a deep breath. *Do I really want to tell him or do I just try to hide* *the truth from him as best I can? After all, he's still traumatized from the assault by those Velociraptors... and they were <u>nothing</u> in comparison to the beast that almost killed him today.* But I realized there was no use making something up... He was going to find out what happened eventually. If I told him now, at least we're all here with him.

I reached out for his hand. "Xander, that thing that attacked Centennial today — That wasn't just a dinosaur," I said.

Xander looked at me, confused. "What do you mean?" he said under knitted brows. "I *saw* it. It was *real!*" he insisted.

"I know you saw it, and it must have been so frightening! What I mean is that the thing was a *GENETICALLY MODIFIED HYBRID*," I said, emphasizing each word.

All the blood rushed out of Xander's face and he looked at me wide-eyed.

"Oh my god!" he cried, shocked.

Sebastian patted Xander's shoulder gently. "It's all right," he said softly. "The thing is dead. We don't have to be afraid of it anymore."

As Xander nodded his head, there was a knock at the door and a nurse carrying IV bags came in, followed by Dr. Lingard, who was consulting his holo as he walked. The nurse went right to Xander and connected the IV tube to the port in his arm. She hung one bag and tapped it to ensure the fluid was flowing right, nodded once, smiled at the doctor and went out the door.

Dr. Lingard looked up from his holo.

"Good afternoon, kids," he said, walking toward us. "I see that my patient is *finally* awake."

When we laughed a little, Xander turned his head and faced me, confused.

"How long have I been asleep?" he asked.

I thought for a moment. "Only about six hours," I said. "But part of that time was thanks to anesthetic."

Placing his hand on Xander's chest, the doctor said, "Yes, you've been out for a while, young man. By the way, I'm Dr. Lingard. Excuse me, gentlemen. If you don't mind, I need to examine my patient."

We took a few steps backward. He walked close to his patient's bedside, pulled down the blankets and opened the front of Xander's hospital gown.

What a horrific sight! All over Xander's chest, dozens of stitches marked where compound fractures of his ribs must have been tucked back under his skin and mended. More stitches traced two long incisions in his abdomen. *Were his intestines torn?* I wondered. *Will he have long-lasting physical problems from what happened to him today?*

"Are you in pain?" Dr. Lingard asked, taking out his stethoscope and starting to check Xander's chest – carefully avoiding areas around the stitches, of course.

"Only a little," Xander said.

"That's really great to hear," the doctor said, pulling his holo from his jacket pocket and tapping in a code…. probably medical shorthand. "But realize that you are still under the last residual effects of the anesthetic. You're going to be subject to quite a lot of pain for a couple of weeks. It'll get easier after that. I expect that you will experience discomfort beginning shortly, but I have ordered medication that you will regulate yourself – just like Daniel did last year. The nurse will set you up as soon as I'm done here." He tapped in more code.

"Can you try touching my hand?" he asked, placing his hand just beyond his patient's reach. Xander positioned his hands on the bed and prepared to push himself a little forward. He hesitated, looking at Sebastian, who got the hint. Sebastian stepped forward and placed his hand on Xander's back, guiding him slowly into a semi-reclining position. Matthew moved up, too, reached over and shoved the pillows forward to prop his friend up as Xander touched the doctor's hand quickly with a fingertip, then relaxed back against the pillows with a big sigh.

"Are you hurting now?" Dr. Lingard asked as he tapped into his holo.

"S-somewhat," Xander said, obviously trying to be brave.

But I could tell that he was hurting a lot more than he let on. *He'll be ready for his pain meds just as soon as the nurse sets them up,* I thought to myself. I remember that feeling from last year!

Dr. Lingard finished tapping in codes, then tucked the holo into his breast pocket.

"I'll look in on you tomorrow," he said. He turned to us. "Gentlemen, you need to let your Teammate rest. Even injured dino hybrids need time to recuperate," he said, heading for the door.

"No… wait, Dr. Lingard," Xander called out. "Sebastian and I aren't dino hybrids. We're just normal kids. We can't morph."

"Well, that's a surprise! I just assumed, since you're here with Daniel and Matthew…" He stopped a moment in thought, then went on, "Well, if Team Triassic has places for non-dino team members, I urge you both – he pointed at Xander and Sebastian – to see if you can join them. You won't be sorry!" He gave a backward wave and went out the door.

Nobody said anything for a very long minute. Then Xander snorted a laugh, cut short by a pain spasm. He breathed in slowly, motioned for Sebastian to come closer, and whispered something to his brother, who nodded eagerly.

"What's going on, you two?" I asked.

Xander turned a bit onto his elbow and faced me. "What do you think about having a set of non-dino *twins* on Team Triassic?" he asked.

I set my chin between my thumb and pointer finger in the classic "thinking" pose. "Hmmmmm… Let me give it some serious consideration," I said, trying to sound very serious. "I'll let you know." But my almost involuntary wink gave away everything.

The nurse came in with an IV bag containing a golden liquid. As she attached it to the IV stand, she explained to Xander that he would be in charge of managing his pain from now on.

"We call this Golden Relief," she said with a grin, showing Xander a small device that resembled a miniature TV remote. Pointing at the four numbers on the device, she explained, "When pain starts to become uncomfortable, press the 1. Wait five minutes. If you don't feel significant relief, press the 2. You can go to 3 if your pain is still too much."

"What's the 4 for?" Sebastian asked, peering at the device.

"That's for nighttime," she said. "It is a sedative dose, and we on the medical staff are usually the ones to administer that level after we make our evening check of his vitals."

Xander winced at a sudden spasm. The nurse handed the little remote to him, and said, "Start with 1."

Xander pressed the 1 and settled back into the pillow. His closed his eyes.

The nurse smiled at us and whispered, "Maybe it's time for all of us to let your friend get some rest." She motioned us toward the door, then remembering something, she turned to me.

"Oh, you're Daniel, aren't you?" she asked.

"Uh- yeah," I said, curious at the question.

"Aurora is requesting to see you," she said. "You know her, right?"

Xander's eyes flew open and he was suddenly awake. "Aurora? Did you say Aurora?" he asked, worried. "She's in my Theater I class – the one we were in when... when that thing... Is she ok?"

I went over and put my hand on his shoulder. "I saw her earlier," I said, leaving out specifics on purpose. "She's ok. She has a nasty gash on her forehead and doctors probably already fixed her dislocated shoulder."

"Dang, that must've hurt. Can I see her?" he asked.

The nurse shook her head. "No, but maybe she'll come to see you in a few days... when you're feeling better." She walked out of the room.

"I can stop by Aurora's room on my way home," I said to Xander. "Is there anything you want me to ask her?"

"No, nothing in par- parti- cular," he said, fading. "I just want to see if my friend..." His eyes closed and he began snoring softly.

Matthew, Sebastian and I tiptoed out of the room, closing the door quietly.

We hit the DOWN button on the elevator. As we waited for it to arrive, we shared our individual plans for the rest of the day.

"I'll probably check in on some of the other kids here in the hospital after I see Aurora," I said.

"I guess I could go to my Grandma's," Sebastian said. "No way do I want to run into Dad."

"No need, Bro," I said. You can come and stay with us. We have lots of room and Mom loves to have extra people to feed. Our house is right on the way to Matthew's, so Nick's dad can drop you. I'll holo-text Mom to expect you."

"Are you SURE it's ok?" Sebastian asked, hesitantly.

"Yep," I said. "See?" I showed him the texts between me and Mom in the last fifteen seconds:

DANIEL: Can Sebastian come to stay with us?

MOM: Sure! Tell him to 'Come on down!'

Matthew was just about to tell us his plans (which we already knew) when a "Yo guys!" from behind us made us stop and turn around. Nick was fast-walking to catch up to us, proudly holding a plastic basket of the hospital's take-home "amenities."

As he fell into step with us, he looked at Matthew and said, "Dude, you ready? My Dad'll be here in about ten minutes, he said."

"Can you drop Sebastian at my house?" I asked Nick.

"No prob. C'mon, both of you," Nick said, gesturing with his basket.

"Thanks," Sebastian said, as the three of them stepped into the elevator. I got on, too, and we rode together to the second floor, where I got off and headed to Aurora's room. I knocked softly.

"Come in!" came a cheery voice.

I peeked around the door.

"Daniel!" she cried. "You came! I didn't know if you would…"

"Why wouldn't I?" I asked, crossing the room and taking a seat next to her bed.

"Oh, I don't know," she said. "You're so busy… and famous!"

"Busy, yes. Famous, I don't think so!" I said with a grin.

"But I just saw the news… The reporter gave you most of the credit for killing the monster and saving lives!" she insisted.

"Yeah, about that… I need to get that corrected. I was just part of my TEAM. And the First Responders were super! We all contributed – EQUALLY. As people say, 'There is no "I" in TEAM!'" I said through clenched teeth, letting out some of the anger I was still feeling.

Aurora's eyes widened and her eyebrows went way up. "Whoa!" she said. "I didn't mean to make you mad."

"Oh, Aurora, I'm sorry. I didn't mean to unload on you. I am just so furious that people who saw that TV broadcast have been given a totally wrong impression about what went on at Centennial today!" I reached over and gave her a light pat on her back.

"I can understand how you feel, Daniel," she said. "Myself… I feel that I didn't do enough today, either."

"What do you mean, Aurora? You were a victim! What could you have done?"

"I wanted to help the injured kids, but I didn't – couldn't — and it makes me sad," she said, looking down.

I reached over with two fingers under her chin and gently raised her face to look at me.

"It's ok. Don't feel bad," I said. "When you're healthy again, I think we'll be able to find lots of ways you can help people."

Just then, Elliott's voice boomed out of my holo.

"I'M STILL WAITING, DANIEL! WHEN ARE YOU PLANNING

TO CONTACT ME? I *DO* HAVE OTHER THINGS TO DO, YOU KNOW!"

Can a computer grit its teeth and cross its arms when speaking? I wondered. *Elliott can get awfully testy!*

I gave Aurora an "I'm sorry" look and turned away to respond to Elliott's cyber-scolding. I tapped in a holo message to my grumpy computer that he should arrange a holo conference with the reporter Chloe for as soon as possible, so I could get this "media-based misunderstanding" fixed.

Now usually, Elliott would respond "Got it" or "OK." This time his return message to me – in a bright red font– was "IT'S ABOUT TIME! EVERYBODY AT HEADQUARTERS IS RILED UP."

Oh no, I thought. *I may have more damage-control to do than I realized.*

"Is anything wrong?" Aurora asked, concerned.

I turned back to her, putting my holo away.

"No… At least I hope everything will be ok. I just need to fix the story with that TV reporter and meet with my Team…"

Aurora nodded, then obviously decided to get my mind off the media problem by changing the subject.

"Do you know Tucker?" she asked, tilting her head.

A little surprised that she would ask about one of the kids I had personally helped to treat in the theater, I said, "Yeah, he's here in the hospital."

"Oh, he is? What's wrong with him… Is it serious? He's a really great friend of mine. Is he ok?"

I thought for a quick second. "Uh, last I heard he was in surgery. I don't know if he's out or not," I said. The image of the pipe impaling Tucker's body flashed through my mind. It was a picture I did *not* want to share with Aurora.

The word "surgery" was all it took to drain all the positive energy out of Aurora. Her eyes teared up.

"I sure hope he's going to be ok," she said, as tears tracked down her cheeks.

"I'm sure he will," I said, not completely believing it. But Aurora needed to have hope, so I said, "He's a tough kid. I saw great spirit in him."

"Well, if you're still here in the hospital when he gets out of surgery and wakes up, can you give him this for me?" she said, holding out some folded sticky-notes. "Here."

I took the notes from her.

"What is it?" I asked.

"It's just telling Tucker that Annie is dead and that I'm joining you guys," she said with an end-of-conversation tone, so I nodded my head and placed the notes in my pocket.

She pulled her covers up to her chin, yawned once and said, "Well, if you don't mind, Daniel, I'm going to take a little nap. It's been a long, scary day." She breathed in deeply and closed her eyes.

Officially "dismissed," I gave her a parting pat on her good shoulder and left her alone.

Stepping into the elevator, I hesitated before hitting "5" for the post-surgical floor where I expected Tucker might be. Then, with sudden inspiration, I hit "6" instead.

Emerging from the elevator, I heard a familiar voice-from-the-past call out, "Hey – Is that you, Daniel?

I turned toward the voice and there stood the strongest little woman I ever knew.

"Emily!" I cried – too loud for a hospital. I ran to give her a hug. In response, she slung that familiar cloth belt around my waist and pulled me in.

"I see that you decided to take a little trip down Memory Lane," she said, "releasing" me and looking over her shoulder at the room that had been my "home" for nearly two months last year.

I laughed a little, realizing she had "caught" me.

"Yeah," I confessed. "I'd like to look around and see if anything's changed," I said. "Is anyone in my old room?"

"Yes," she said. "A young man named William. Came in today from the Centennial attack. Dr. Miller is taking care of him," she said.

"Oh, wait… Did you say William?" I asked. "Do you know if he has short blond hair?"

"Why yes…, yes, he does. And *really* blue eyes."

"I know that kid!" I said, excitedly. "I helped him out earlier today. Can I peek in and see him?"

Just then Dr. Miller came out of William's room.

"Serendipity!" Emily said, taking me by the hand to meet the doctor. She quickly filled him in on me and my request to see William.

"The nurse is with him at the moment, making him comfortable and setting up his meds," Dr. Miller said. "But as soon as you see her come out of his room, go ahead and knock and see if he's wanting to see you." His holo sounded and he was off down the hall.

"Thank you, Dr. Miller," I called, trying not to be too loud.

"Of course!" he called back over his shoulder.

Emily hung out with me as I waited for my – William's – door to open. We sat on a bench together a few doors down the hallway.

"I remember all the therapy we did with you in that room – and down this hallway," she said with a little laugh.

I laughed with her. "Yeah, you put me through hell," I said.

"So how's your leg doing? Did Dr. Lingard leave you a nice-looking scar to remember it all?" she asked with a wink.

I backed up on the bench so I could extend my left leg between us. As I leaned down to roll up my pants and reveal the scar to Emily, a familiar voice interrupted us.

"Did I hear that someone wants to evaluate my talent as a surgical seamstress?"

Dr. Lingard had emerged from a nearby patient's room and strode over to us. I looked up and laughed, pulling my pant leg up to my left knee, revealing the long scar.

Emily smiled. "Pretty!" she said.

Dr. Lingard leaned close. "'Pretty?' I don't know about 'pretty,'" he said. "It's acceptable, I guess." He ran his finger along the full twelve inches, nodding every four inches or so. "It's got that nice little ridge to it!" he said.

"I like it very much because it makes me look tough," I said, grinning.

Dr. Lingard stood up and patted me on the shoulder. "You don't need to 'look tough,' Daniel," he said. "You ARE tough. You proved that last year!" A beep from his holo called him away, and he took off toward the elevator with a backward wave and a "See you later!"

Emily reached over and touched my scar lightly. Her hands were cold, and I jumped a little from the shock.

"Sorry Daniel," she apologized. She rubbed her hands together to warm them up, then reached out to trace the line of my scar as Dr. Lingard had done.

"Beautiful work," she said, impressed.

I laughed. "It's come a long way," I said. "Every day when I shower, I look at that scar and realize that if it hadn't been for Dr. Lingard, I probably wouldn't have had my leg anymore... or maybe I wouldn't be here today at all," I said. Emily reached up and gave me a hug.

Just then, the door to William's room opened and the nurse came out, heading down the hall away from us. Emily and I said our farewells and headed in opposite directions. I knocked on the door of room 617.

Chapter 38

"Come in!" that very cultured-sounding young voice called out.

I opened the door to a room that looked exactly as I remembered it… except the bed contained a lanky blond boy, not me. He clicked off the TV as I entered.

This kid has manners, I thought to myself.

"Hi, William," I said. "Remember me? I'm Daniel from Team Triassic. I stopped in to see you a little while ago. Are you up for another visit? "

"Are you really THAT Daniel?" he cried, pressing a remote to bring him to a comfortable sitting position. "No kidding? I didn't realize before that you were… YOU!"

I walked over to his bed side. "No kidding!" I said, grinning. "Do you think you can tell me about what happened today?" I asked him.

"Sure," he said. "But I don't remember a lot." He looked off to his right, thinking for a few seconds.

"What I do remember is that I was in seventh period, Theatre class. Mrs. Carter had asked Tucker and me to go upstairs and work on the lights. Xander was already up there doing something with the overhead speakers, I think. So that's where we all were. I was adjusting one of the kliegs when I heard a roar and felt the whole room shake. Xander was walking on a catwalk behind us, and he suddenly went flying across the theater. That's when I saw the weird dinosaur that had crashed through the auditorium wall – right where Xander had been. Tucker and I started to run toward the stairs to get out of there. Then the floor gave way under us and… and…" He stopped.

"And?" I asked, encouraging him to go on. This was really valuable information!

"That's all I remember," he said, shaking his head sadly. "I don't know what happened after that. I woke up in an ambulance."

"Wow," I said, breathing out slowly. "William, I'm so sorry that this happened to you."

He shook his head, maybe to rid his mind of the unpleasantness. Then he looked at me and grinned widely.

"I don't really mind if I have injuries to my body. It's my brain that is most important to me. As long as I can still study genetics, I'm fine," he said with a firm nod of his head.

"You study genetics?" I asked, surprised.

His grin widened even more. "Absolutely!" he said, and there was definite pride in his voice. "It's been my primary interest since I was eleven, so I read everything that I can get my hands on. I want to become a genetics scientist someday," he said.

"Do you get to *do* anything nowadays that's associated with your interest?" I asked, as an idea was quickly forming in my mind.

"Well, no, not really… People think I'm just a kid. I think I know a lot, but not too many ninth-graders get the chance to work in a real lab," he pointed out, sarcastically.

"Would you *want* to work in a genetics research lab if you could?" I asked casually.

"WOULD I?! Are you kidding me? It would be like… like every one of my dreams come true!" he cried, full of excitement. But in an instant, reality settled into his mind and the excitement vanished. "Too bad it's not possible… I just have to wait," he said, sadly.

"What if it *were* possible?" I asked him, looking him full in the face. "It just so happens that my Dad is Dr. Christopher Robertson. You may have heard of him…"

"*Dr. Robertson?!*" he shrieked. "He's been my hero my whole life! He's *your DAD?*"

I thought he was about to jump out of his bed, which would probably not have been good for his injuries, so I put out both hands in a "Calm down" gesture and spoke in a very low, measured tone.

"William, here's what we're going to do. When you are out of the hospital and feeling up to it, I'll arrange for you to meet Dad up at his lab on Lone Mountain. He may have a spot for you. I know he's always saying how he can never get to all the experiments he wants to do, so having a young intern might appeal to him. I'll speak to him over the weekend."

He looked thrilled, then suddenly wary. "I wouldn't have to do any fighting, like your Team does, right?" he asked, warily, explaining, "I'm a pacifist."

"Nope!" I said. "The research and the Team Triassic facilities share a footprint, but other than that, we have completely different missions. The two facilities do have a symbiotic relationship, though. Your genetic research with Dad might actually help us on Team Triassic. Your 'fighting' would be through the use of test tubes and petri dishes, not dino claws and jaws," I said, smiling at my semi-poetic cleverness.

"That sounds... FABULOUS! You're serious about this?" he asked, breathlessly. When I smiled and nodded, he sighed deeply and said, "Now, I REALLY can't wait to get out of this hospital!"

I realized that he should be resting – and he was so excited that "resting" was definitely *not* what he was doing — so I took the initiative to get out of there.

"Hey, William," I said, as though I just remembered something, "I was on my way to check in on Tucker..."

"Tucker?" he cried. "Is he here? I didn't know that he was hurt. Is he ok? He's one of my best friends!"

Hmmmm, I thought... *This Tucker must be some special kid. Two 'best friends' are worried about him.*

Backing away from his bed, I said, "I know he was in surgery a couple of hours ago, but I haven't heard since. I'll let you know if I learn anything. You rest. I'll catch you later."

Before we could get involved in anymore conversation, I made a beeline for the door and left William alone in "my" room.

The elevator stopped at 5 and I got out. Since I wasn't sure if Tucker would actually have ended up as Xander's roommate on this "post-op" floor, I walked over to the Nurses Station. A very overweight nurse was standing with her back to me, consulting a bank of computers. I waited patiently for her to notice me. When more than three minutes passed, I cleared my throat to get her attention.

"Excuse me. Nurse?"

She turned around slowly. "Y-esss?"

"Could you please tell me what room Tucker is in? I'm afraid I don't know his last name, but I have an important message for him – if he's out of surgery," I said, holding up the folded pack of sticky notes.

One heavily penciled eyebrow dipped as she looked over at the notes, but her customer service training kicked in and she crossed the station to take a seat in her rolling chair. Pulling herself up to the desk, she said, "Tucker? Is he a student from Centennial High School?"

I nodded my head. "Yes, ma'am. Is he out of surgery?"

"Yes, he's just out of Recovery. Are you a relative?"

I was a little surprised at the question, since I had already told her I didn't know Tucker's last name, but I decided just to identify myself and give her some "credentials."

"No, I'm not a relative. I'm Daniel Robertson of Team Triassic. I've been helping hospital staff with some of the Centennial High victims today. You can check with Dr. Lingard or Dr. Miller."

Her perfectly arched eyebrows now went way up on her forehead. Without a word to me, she pressed numbers on her handset and turned away to speak quietly on the phone. A number of nods and "Uh-huhs" later, she turned back around with a brand-new, big smile.

"Mr. Robertson, the doctor says Tucker Gilbert has been moved into room 519, down the hall to your left. It is not our normal procedure for non-relatives to visit patients just out of surgery, but Dr. Lingard has given you his personal permission, so that's that." She got up, crossed the station and returned to what she had been doing before my interruption.

I walked down the long hallway to what I considered "Xander's room," 519. The door was closed, so I tapped lightly. When there was no answer, I opened the door and poked in my head. The privacy curtain was pulled around where I knew Xander's bed was, so I walked quietly to the bed across the room, where I could see a very still form covered chin-high with a blue blanket. Wires and tubes connected him to a tiered set of monitors and an IV stand with two bags of clear fluid. (No Golden Relief, I noted.) I made my way to an upholstered chair under the window and sat down to wait for Tucker to wake up. I closed my eyes to relax after what had been a very busy, emotional day.

"Hey!"

I jumped, instantly awake. I looked at my chrono and was shocked. It was 8:13! *I must have napped in this chair for over three hours!*

"Hey! You… Daniel!" His voice was raspy but very insistent.

"Oh hey, Tucker. How do you feel?" I asked.

He looked at me with a face that said it all. As an answer to my question, he uncovered his arms and pushed the blanket down to his upper thighs. When he opened his hospital robe, I was relieved to see they had put him in post-op paper undershorts, as I had been a little leery to see "too much" of this guy I hardly knew. Gingerly, he pulled away the corner of a large bandage on the left side of his abdomen where I remembered the pipe had poked through. We could see a few of the stitches that had already oozed through the bandage in a red C-shaped line. I expected that a similar incision was stitched up and bandaged on his back where the pipe entered, and there were probably lots of stitches inside repairing the internal damage.

"Ouch!" I said, with empathetic pain in my voice.

"It's starting to hurt a lot," he said, breathlessly. "I think the anesthetic is wearing off."

I couldn't imagine the pain he must be in. "Are you under some pain meds?" I asked him.

He shrugged his shoulders. "If I am, they're not working," he said, wincing.

"Let's call the nurse," I said. The words were no sooner out of my mouth than a cute young nurse came through the door with an IV bag full of golden fluid.

"I think it's time that we switch your saline to some Golden Relief," she said, smiling. "Your monitors tell me your pain level is rising… right?"

He nodded, and I realized that he was actually unable to speak because the pain was getting so bad.

The nurse quickly explained the 1-2-3-4 buttons on the pain med remote and pressed 1. "If this doesn't help in five minutes, go ahead and press 2," she told him. She straightened up his bedding, gathered up used supplies and left the room.

I felt so bad for this kid. Did I really want to give the sticky-note letter to him now and reveal what happened to his friend? I was still pondering this dilemma when I heard Tucker sigh deeply.

"Daniel," he said, weakly, "Do you know anything about Aurora? Is Aurora ok?"

I closed my eyes for a quick second. Here we go, I decided.

"Yeah, she's ok. Same thing with William. And Aurora asked me to give this to you," I said, handing him the folded sticky-notes.

He shook his head. "I can't read without my glasses," he said.

I looked around for a pair of glasses, opened the bedside chest drawer, but found nothing.

"Can you read it for me?" he asked.

My heart sank to my stomach. I sighed, wanting to say, "No, just wait until you have your glasses," but I knew that was not going to happen.

"Yeah, I can read it for you," I said. I opened the first note and started reading out loud.

Hey Tucker, it's Aurora. I'll be there to visit you as soon as I can. I'm very heartbroken to tell you Annie has been killed by that crazy dinosaur.

I stopped reading and looked up at Tucker. His eyes filled with tears and his mouth dropped open a little. I kept reading.

I just finished talking to Daniel. He's the leader of Team Triassic. I asked if I could join the Team. You should, too, when you're healed. I know that we both like to help people. And we can do it for Annie.

I finished reading, folded the notes and handed them to Tucker.

"About Annie," he asked, haltingly. "Was it quick? She didn't suffer, did she?"

"I can't answer that because I don't know," I said. "But a lot of the serious injuries happened from falling cement or other sudden things, so maybe she…" I stopped, not knowing how to phrase it. "Probably it *was* quick," I finished.

I pulled my chair closer to Tucker's bedside and placed my hand on his shoulder.

"I'm sorry," I said.

He shook his head no. "It's not your fault. But about honoring Annie by joining Team Triassic…" He stopped for a few seconds, wincing in pain, then started again. "About joining Team Triassic… Aurora would be a good addition to your team, I think. Her genome is a *Triceratops* — pretty powerful, I think. Do you have one of those?" He winced again, then reached over and pressed 2 on his pain remote.

He took a deep breath and continued his thought. "I've been told my dino hybrid is a tiny *Confuciusornus*, so I probably couldn't help much… even if I heal to 100%."

"You'd be surprised," I said. "My brother Andy is an *Avian Sinustrodon* – not much bigger than a California condor – and what he did today saved lots of lives. Aurora's *Triceratops* AND your *Confuciusornus* would be able to make significant contributions to Team Triassic… *if* you decide to come on board."

He smiled, and he seemed about to say something else when his 2-level Golden Relief must have kicked in. His eyes closed and his breathing slowed to a deep, regular tempo as he drifted off to Dreamland.

I took this opportunity to get out of the hospital – finally. I holo-texted Mom, asking for a ride. Within 30 seconds, the return-holo dinged.

MOM Be there in 20

I guess she misses me, I thought, smiling. The elevator took me down to ground level and I walked across the ER and through the exit door, happy to be out in the familiar smog-filled air of the city.

Dear Diary,

OMG! I screwed up so badly today! Everybody at Headquarters is mad at me because of what I said on TV. I didn't mean anything by it, but no one wants to believe that. I was just so blown away by how HEROIC Daniel always is – and he's usually so humble – that I just wanted him to get credit for what he does.

When I got back to Headquarters, everything was normal. Kayla, Juli, Johnny and I were all talking about how the day turned out and how great the Team worked together. This was the first real test of our training for the last few months, so we didn't know how good we'd be. But we were awesome! We kept the dino attack from being worse than it was. (And it was <u>really</u> horrible. I still can't believe that people actually DIED today.)

We were all there in the Control Room, checking monitors, tracking Team members on location and watching for other rogue dinos (like always), when Action News came on. Ten minutes later, everything had changed. The look on Kayla's face as my interview went on was one of growing rage. Juli looked stunned. I thought Johnny was ready to smack me. As I watched myself on TV, I got more and more embarrassed and very annoyed at myself for letting my feelings for Daniel spill out in front of the camera. And I was horrified that I OVERLOOKED the courageous efforts of all of the other Team members. I made it sound like a "one-man show," and it certainly was not that.

After my interview was over, Johnny stormed out of the Control Room, slamming the door. I tried to explain to Kayla and Juli that the reporter caught me off-guard, that I didn't have time to plan what I was going to say... but they didn't want to hear it. Juli said, "So much for teamwork!" and followed Johnny out of the Control Room. Kayla said, "Well, I hope you and Daniel will be very happy together!" and she left, too. Within five minutes everybody at Headquarters had heard about what I did.

Now I'm worried what the other Team members will think of me. And – even more important – what Daniel will think if he sees my interview. I can only hope he's too busy at the hospital to watch the News. Oh, what am I saying? He'll definitely learn about it from <u>somebody</u>. I wonder if he'll kick me off the Team. I am so scared!

Lynnelle

Chapter 42

Mom pulled the Mercedes up to the curb right in front of me and I climbed into its smog-free interior. She reached over and gave me a one-armed hug.

"Quite a tough day you've had, Sweetheart," she said, with concern clouding her face. "Are you ok?"

"Yeah, *I'm* ok," I said, emphasizing the "I." But nine kids will *never* be ok again and a couple of dozen others won't be ok for quite a while. It's not like last year, when Nick had some scrapes and had to have a few stitches..."

"And YOU were in a coma for 33 days and almost lost your leg – AND your life!" Mom reminded me, in her Mama Bear persona.

"I know, I know," I said. "It was bad for me, but I came out of it. No one DIED. Today was so much worse! The only good thing out of it all was that everybody on the Team did a fantastic job. I can't imagine how many more people would have become victims of that dino if Team Triassic had not been there. I am so proud of all of them!"

Mom looked puzzled. "You say that *everybody* on Team Triassic was involved at Centennial High?" she asked. "That's not what they're saying on the News. The only person named was you, son," she said, looking at me from under lowered brows.

"THAT'S NOT HOW IT WAS!" I roared, and I could see my "stress morphing" beginning on both hands. I quickly started my deep breathing, but I was really upset. The white discoloration and scaling continued to grow.

Mom looked over at me with alarm. Was I about to burst her Mercedes to pieces by morphing into my full-extension dino in the passenger seat? We were passing Mountain View Park just then, so she quickly pulled over. I got out and took off at a run for the park's restroom. Inside a stall in the Men's Room, I tried to calm myself. It took over ten minutes of my breathing routine before my arms de-morphed and I could get back to Mom, waiting in the car.

"OK now?" she asked, as I climbed in.

"Yep," I said, "but there's something I need to do the minute we get home."

"I think I might know what it's about," she said. Pointing to my holo in the car's console, she explained, "Elliott has been calling you the whole time you were in the restroom. He said you have a holo call with some woman named Chloe in twenty minutes. Is that the same Chloe from the News?"

At the mention of the reporter's name, I felt stress coming on again.

"Mom, we need to get home... NOW!" I said, trying to breathe deeply as I spoke.

"Three minutes," she said, pressing down the gas pedal. We swung into our driveway in two minutes-ten and I took off upstairs, stripping my clothes as I ran. I knew I needed to get at least some of the day's dirt and sweat off me before I faced Chloe. I turned on the water and jumped into the shower, shivering a little as the water took too long to heat up, then stepping into the rain-shower when it reached just the right temperature. I scrubbed my body quickly, shampooed my hair and rinsed off, standing still under the water for about five minutes. Breathing deeply, I could feel the stress leaving my body. *I am SO glad we have this rain shower!* I thought.

By the time my holo call appointment time came, I was clean, calm and cool as the proverbial cucumber. And dressed, of course, in one of my "business casual" outfits – a red polo shirt and khaki shorts. No shoes (but I didn't think the camera would be filming my feet).

Elliott gave me his usual "HEADS UP! YOU HAVE AN APPOINTMENT IN THREE MINUTES!" So I settled at the table in front of our large two-way wall screen. Mom sneaked into the room and slid a chilled bottle of water across the table to me.

"Good luck!" she whispered. She went out, turned the corner and was out of sight.

I waited in front of the blank screen, wondering just how *this* interview with Chloe Simpson would turn out.

Overnight, I received holos from Kayla and Juli, asking for an emergency Team meeting in the morning, and Lynnelle sent me one that said simply "I'm so sorry!"… so things were probably messed up. And when Elliott dinged me about the meeting scheduled for "NINE AM PROMPTLY," he sounded even crosser than usual.

In the morning I turned on *Action News* at 7:30 with a worried feeling. I *thought* my interview with Chloe the night before had gone the way I hoped it would, but you never can tell… With all the cutting and editing they do, I could have ended up saying the exact opposite of what I *thought* I said.

When the morning anchor, Kevin Fowler, introduced "my colleague Chloe Simpson," I found myself holding my breath. Fowler said, "Chloe has a follow-up to her report yesterday from the site of the Centennial High School devastation. We understand that some clarification of details is in order. Chloe?"

"Thank you, Kevin," the reporter said to the camera. "Yes, I had the opportunity last evening to meet via holo with young Daniel Robertson, the co-founder of Team Triassic. Daniel was eager to clarify some details about the clash between his Team and the rogue dinosaur responsible for death and devastation at Centennial High. I asked him to share his perspective, and here's what he said…"

Chloe's image moved left to share a split-screen with me. I have to admit that I looked pretty uncomfortable staring straight ahead. I must have been given a cue then, because I glanced to my right, hesitated a second, and then started speaking into the camera. The reporter's image dissolved and it was all me on the screen.

"Thank you, Ms. Simpson, for this opportunity to acknowledge everyone who took part in fighting the rogue dinosaur at Centennial High. Every member of Team Triassic and all the First Responders played their heroic parts in limiting the carnage. I want to recognize the efforts of our Headquarters team, Kayla St. Pierre and Juli Anderson, who alerted our Team to the approach of two rogue dinosaurs and then coordinated the offensive by my Co-Leader Nick Williamson and me and our squad of dino hybrids – Angel Williamson, Matthew Williams, Timeer Biggs, Michael Watanabe, Johnny Castelletti and my brother Andy Robertson – ALL employing our individual strengths that led to the death of the beast, as Lynnelle McPherson and others led many students out of the theater to safety. And I cannot say enough about the First Responders whose quick actions and professional expertise saved the wounded, many of whom have been receiving treatment by the excellent staffs at Centennial Hills and Desert Springs Hospitals.

"This violent attack was something that none of us wanted to happen, of course, but we members of Team Triassic have been working every day for months in coordination with police and First Responders to meet the challenge of such an attack. We members of our Team send our thoughts and prayers to the families of those who lost their lives and to the many injured students who are recovering from their injuries.

"In conclusion, I'll say that all of us on Team Triassic want the people of Las Vegas to know that we will continue to prepare to meet every future assault wherever and whenever it threatens the people of our city. Thank you."

My image disappeared and Chloe filled the screen.

"So there you have it," she said, nodding her head once. "KTLV is always pleased to set the record straight and give all our local heroes the recognition they deserve. Thank you, Mr. Robertson. Back to you, Kevin, in the studio."

I clicked off the wall screen and just sat there for a few minutes, trying to remember my every word and analyzing what I said. Was it enough?

Too much? Would my interview make things at Headquarters – and with the First Responders, too – better, worse… or?

Mom poked her head in the door with a question on her face.

"Well?" she said, waiting.

"I don't know," I said. "It seemed ok, but what matters is what the Team took in from what I said. I guess I'll know soon enough."

I checked my chrono – 7:50 – and gathered my things off the table.

"Taking a shower," I told Mom. "Back in fifteen. Are you making breakfast this morning?"

Mom smiled. "Of course! You need pancakes and breakfast sausage to prepare you for your day. And fresh pineapple! Dad's already at the table. I'll let him know you'll join him soon."

"Thanks, Mom," I said, heading upstairs.

Chapter 44

Having breakfast with Dad gave the two of us a chance to "catch up" with what happened yesterday and with things in general. He was horrified to hear my account of the attack, but he said he was proud of me – both for dealing with the attack and for helping at the hospital. That made me feel good.

"You know that call you told me to expect from Dr. Lingard?" he said, spearing a piece of pancakes stacked three-high. He hovered his fork-full in front of his mouth, as he continued, "Well, he called me last night about 9 o'clock and we set things up for day after tomorrow. I'll have a couple of free hours to show him around. Looking forward to it!" Then he was happily chewing a mouthful of pancakes.

"Great, Dad," I said enthusiastically. "Let me know how it goes."

"Why don't you join us – if you can get away, that is," he suggested. "My office, 10 o'clock sharp."

"Thanks, Dad, I will," I said.

I stood up, gave him a hug and took my already-empty plate to the kitchen. (I eat FAST!) As I walked to get my things ready for the day, I felt good about my breakfast with Dad and even maybe about my TV interview.

Mom was waiting in the driveway to run me to Lone Mountain. As I climbed into the car, she asked, "Good start for the day?"

"I think so," I said. "Thanks for the pancakes and the pineapple.

Whatever I face this morning on the mountain, at least I am well-fed," I said, grinning.

As it turned out, I needn't have worried about what I'd face at Headquarters. Mom and I were just approaching the gate when Elliott came onto my wrist holo.

"DANIEL, ALL IS WELL AT HEADQUARTERS. THE TEAM HELD A PRE-MEETING-MEETING AT 8 O'CLOCK – YOU WERE NOT INFORMED ON PURPOSE – AND EVERY ONE WATCHED BOTH LYNNELLE'S INTERVIEW AND YOURS. THE ISSUE IS NOW CLOSED WITH HUGS ALL AROUND AND THE 9 O'CLOCK MEETING IS CANCELLED. TIME TO GET BACK TO WORK!"

Mom and I looked at each other, speechless. Then she said, "Now, THAT'S the way a real Team handles problems. You have assembled top-notch kids, Daniel. Your Dad and I are so proud of you! Now, get out of the car and make more magic happen!"

Elliott had already opened the gate for me, so I strode right into the complex, the biggest grin on my face. This was going to be a really good day... I could feel it!

Chapter 45

Since the 9 o'clock meeting was cancelled, I just wandered around for about a half-hour from one cubicle or office to another, stopping to talk to anyone I ran into along the way. Each person I met made it a point to tell me that everything was ok with the Team, that yesterday's "unpleasantness" was a thing of the past, and that everybody wanted to concentrate on whatever work they had scheduled "so we don't lose momentum." (I figured that Lynnelle probably chose that phrase in their Pre-Meeting-Meeting, since she is our resident wordsmith and a number of Team members used that same term.)

Whatever. Nobody needed me urgently – or really at all – so I decided to stop in to Dad's lab to check on his analysis of the samples Johnny delivered to him. I was very curious about what those two dinos were made of.

Dad was bent over a high-powered electron microscope when I entered the lab. I waited a minute so as not to disturb him in the midst of something important, then walked up closer.

"Hey Dad," I said.

He turned. "Oh, there you are. I've been working on the samples Johnny dropped off," he said. "They are proving to be VERY interesting!"

"How so?" I asked.

"Well, each sample I have run through my Base Genome Reader has overloaded the machine."

I gasped. "Why do you think that's happening, Dad?" I asked, worried.

"Think of it this way," he began, adopting a tutorial tone. "The BGR can identify up to four genomes in one sample, and that is usually plenty for the research I do routinely. But these samples overburden the machine's software, so it turns itself off after it has identified four genomes."

"So what can you do?" I inquired, now more concerned.

"Oh, not to worry," Dad said. "I just moved down the counter here to a more advanced apparatus, the AGR – for Advanced Genome Reader, of course – and *Voila!* The samples you provided have been popping up with DNA markers of dinosaurs found all over the world! Somebody went to a LOT of trouble to assemble them to create one new dino hybrid."

"Wow!" I said.

"But that's not the weirdest thing, Daniel," Dad said, looking me right in the eyes.

"What is the weirdest thing, Dad?" I asked, feeling a little weird myself suddenly.

"Daniel, both of these samples have one thing in common… Their base genome is *your* dino hybrid, the one I created for you in the old GAR when you were three days old," he said.

"What!? How is that even possible?" I asked, shocked.

"I can't say how it happened, but look for yourself." He leaned back from the display panel of the AGR and tilted it toward me. There was no doubt. On the monitor in front of me was the graphic image of my dino hybrid's "recipe."

"What? How?" I sputtered. Then in a flash, I knew how it happened.

"Dad, it's Julian!" I said, absolutely convinced. I flashed back to that night last year when Julian sneaked into my hospital room and took blood from my arm. *Could Julian be behind this? Is he still out there somewhere in our city?* Since no one had seen him for the last year, I had hoped he and his family had left Las Vegas. But maybe not.

"I think Julian is behind this," I said.

Dad looked at me and stood up straight. "Julian? I haven't heard about that kid in a long time. I thought he left town," Dad said. "Didn't we find his house deserted that morning on our way to the Molasky celebration?"

"Yes, we did, but I guess he's back," I said, angrily.

Dad put his hands on my shoulders and spoke directly. "You and everyone on the Team will stop him, right?" he asked, obviously expecting only a positive response.

"Of course, we can take *Julian* down. He's not even a dino... or at least, he *wasn't* one," I said. "But we don't know who he – and probably his Dad – have been working with. And what other experimental dino hybrids they have that are ready to go. Those are the real issues."

"Well, I have faith in you. You'll do the right thing, son," he said, giving me a pat. He started to turn back to his work, but I stopped him. I didn't feel that I knew enough about the beast whose samples were under analysis.

"What specific other genomes WERE these two hybrids made of, Dad?" I asked, peering at the small images on the screen.

Dad pressed some buttons and the images changed. "It appears that they have the cranium of a *Pachycephalosaurus*," he said.

I nodded my head a little. "I guess that's how the one was able to smash through the school so easily. What about the arms? They don't look normal for a *Pachycephalosaurus* or for my genome," I said.

He scanned the monitor to the arms area. It showed that it was made of my genome partly, but there were traits of *Velociraptor* limbs and it had *Therizinosaurus* claws. Its body was a lot like my *T-Rex* with a row of *Stegosaurus*-like plates running down its spine. Its hide was armor-plated, except on its belly.

"Here's an interesting wrinkle," Dad said, pulling up on-screen the holos Johnny had taken of the two dead beasts. Notice anything about their tails?" he asked.

I leaned forward to look closely. "Well, they look a little like the clublike tail of an *Ankylosaurus*," I said, "but they're lop-sided... or somewhat deformed."

"Right," Dad said, "but compare this holo to this one," he pointed at the dino that died before the attack and then at the one that attacked the theater. "What's different about the tails?"

"We-ll," I stalled, hoping some of Dad's genius would slide over to me. Then it hit me! "The tail of the first one is deformed to the left and the second one is deformed to the right... right?" I asked, excitedly, my eyebrows up almost to my hairline.

"Right!" Dad said, and he gave me a resounding pat on the back.

"These two animals were obviously somebody's attempt to create 'mirror twins.' We have them in our human species, too, but they are rare," Dad explained. "Mirror twins are identical, except one will be left-handed and one right-handed. And often their brains are mirrors, too... One will be creative and one will be analytical. One will be more introverted and one will be an extrovert. I think the scientist who created these twins was hoping to 'cover all the bases' when it came to designing the ultimate thinking-fighting machines!"

"And you can tell all this from two deformed tails?" I asked, finding all this really hard to take in.

"Well, it's an indicator," Dad said. "Often a small thing like a tail deformity lets us look for other problems in a created species. I remember one guinea pig experiment years ago when I added a longevity gene from a parrot. The guinea pig's hair turned green and the animal died after two weeks. Only on post-mortem did I learn that the guinea pig's esophagus had atrophied—because a parrot does not need one."

"Wow!" I said, impressed.

"So the deformed tail could lead us to any number of other things. This is going to be one very interesting analysis!" he said, and he sounded pretty excited. "Oh, and by the way, these animals were completely nocturnal until you first saw them in the daytime this week. Why they switched to diurnal is something else for me to study."

He sat back down in front of his analyzing equipment and spun a couple of dials with a flourish (for my benefit, I think). But his carefree demeanor screeched to a halt when the dial settled on "SIZE AT MATURITY." He gasped in shock.

I looked at him. "What?"

All the blood seemed to have rushed out of his face. In a quiet, halting voice, he said, "These dino hybrids were genetically altered to be *bigger than you* at full growth!" he said, shaking his head. He turned to look at me. "I guess we have to consider ourselves lucky – in a way – that those two yesterday were sent to attack when they were probably only 'teenagers.' AND that they got into a brotherly tiff before they attacked. Who knows what a massacre they could have carried out if they had been full-grown and working together!"

That realization struck me dumb. For a few minutes I was literally incapable of speech. When I finally came to myself, I just had to ask – considering that this was Dad, after all: "So… what would you name this thing?" I asked.

He rested his chin in his hand, looked off to the right corner of the ceiling and thought a moment. "Well," he said, "Its name has to show that it's bigger than *Regem Insuperabilus*, and we don't want to use either 'unbeatable' or the Roman 'king' from your name," he began.

I had a sudden inspiration. "*Gigantosupersaurus Rex!*" I shouted.

He nodded his head. "Interesting!" he said, before tapping the name onto the monitor. As he keyed the new name into his Master Directory, he scared me to death by commenting matter-of-factly, "I don't know why this creature was made, but I do know that it was made only to kill," he said.

Again, I didn't know what to say.

Dad went on, seeming to be talking almost to himself. "It's a true killing machine. Good thing the Team was able to stop it before it killed everyone in that auditorium," he said.

I nodded my head a little, but still it had to be said: "I know, Dad, but those dead kids had so much ahead of them. They were so innocent. And some of the other kids will suffer their whole lives because of their injuries." I had to hold my breath to keep from crying.

"You and the Team did everything you could yesterday," Dad said to me, patting my shoulder.

"Yeah, I know. But what happened yesterday – and the very idea that more of the same could be coming – Well, we just have to push ourselves to greater limits," I said, meaning it 100%.

Chapter 46

Dear Diary,

What a difference a day makes! Last night I felt so terrible and I thought the whole team hated me for what I said on TV. I know I gave Daniel too much individual credit for killing that dino and saving kids, but he is SO AWESOME that I just couldn't help myself. And I didn't realize how mad and hurt Kayla, Juli and the guys would feel. I have to learn to be more careful and thoughtful. And maybe to get better at hiding how I feel about Daniel.

We were supposed to have a Team meeting at 9 today, but we all got an "update" from Elliott at 7 this morning, telling us the meeting would be at 8 instead. What we didn't know until we got to the conference room was that Nick had called the earlier meeting and he hadn't told Daniel about it. At first, this seemed really WRONG... going behind Daniel's back ... but Nick said he wanted us all together to "mend fences" by watching both my interview and one that Daniel did later with the same reporter. So that's what we did. I have to admit that my heart skipped a beat when Daniel was speaking. He looked so handsome!

After both interviews were over, Nick turned off the wall screen, crossed his arms, stared at each of us and asked us one question: "Has what happened yesterday – the attack <u>and</u> the interviews – damaged the Team?" We all looked at each other. I was afraid to say anything, so I was relieved when Kayla was first to say "No, not at all" followed by Johnny's "No way!" and the same kind of response from everybody else. When it was my turn, I just shook my head no, since I was afraid I'd start to cry if I tried to say anything.

Then Nick said, "Let's all learn from this, ok? Going forward... Rule 1: Avoid talking with reporters unless the interview is planned and you have been given Talking Points by Daniel or me. Rule 2: Always think the BEST of our Teammates <u>first</u>. Give each other the benefit of the doubt. Rule 3: We have no time for drama in Team Triassic. Our mandate is too critical. Especially after what we experienced yesterday, we must re-dedicate every bit of our talents and abilities to protecting the people of Las Vegas. So... Are we all together? TEAM TRIASSIC!"

Everybody jumped up and flew into a huge group hug. Somehow I was in the middle, so I felt that everybody was hugging ME. It was awesome!

We all started heading out to our scheduled jobs when I saw Nick hastily tapping a message into the conference table holo. Elliott's voice came back, "WILL DO," so I assumed Nick had told Elliott to inform Daniel about what just happened. When Nick headed to his office, I hung around outside the door long enough to overhear Elliott telling Daniel, "THE ISSUE IS NOW CLOSED WITH HUGS ALL AROUND."

I was so relieved. But I also felt re-energized. I think I got more work done on our new self-defense program for non-hybrids in this one day than I had in any other THREE days!

Thank you, Nick! (By the way, his new haircut almost evens out the left side shaved in the hospital with the rest of his head. But he sure looks different!)

Lynnelle

I surprised myself at how excited I was that Dr. Lingard was going to be visiting Dad's lab. The night before his 10 a.m. appointment, I hardly slept a wink. And when I did sleep, I had all sorts of "flashback-type" dreams about my fight with the *SpinoRex* last year. The worst one was a replay of my nightmare, where a massive attack of rogue dino hybrids had destroyed much of Las Vegas and killed hundreds of people, including Dr. Lingard. I woke up in a cold sweat after that one and decided to stay awake the rest of the night. It was 4:47 a.m.

With time on my hands, I resolved to do something purely for fun. What I settled on would also be a completely unexpected surprise for Kayla and Juli, who have been juggling their Team assignments with play rehearsals for weeks, with not one complaint. I decided to learn two songs from "Annie Get Your Gun," both of which had Kayla or Juli singing with one or more other singers. I would be their "other singers."

I started with "Doin' What Comes Natur'lly," which they both sing with their siblings in the play. It took a little research to learn who sang which lines, but I eventually figured it out. And my sometimes-cracking voice actually added a realism to my part as one of Annie's brothers.

"Anything You Can Do, I Can Do Better" has always been a favorite song of mine, so I just needed to remind myself of the order of topics in Annie's musical squabble with Frank and practice the higher and higher notes as the vocal spat intensified. I had my door closed through all of this – and my room is way on the other side of the house from Dad and Mom's room – so I was not expecting to see Dad's head poke inside my door at 5:50 a.m. (He is not a morning person.)

"Are you... SINGING?" he asked, rubbing his eyes. "It's not even light yet!"

"Oh, sorry, Dad. I was just trying to kill time since I couldn't sleep. I'm pretty excited about Dr. Lingard coming to Lone Mountain today."

"So you're SINGING before dawn?"

"Well, Kayla and Juli both have parts in the Spring Mountain Little Theater production of 'Annie Get Your Gun,'" I told him, "and they have been working so hard to keep up with Team jobs while having rehearsals that I thought I'd surprise them by helping them run lines for their songs. Besides, to tell the truth, I really miss being in Theater."

"Well, how about this..." he said, struggling to suppress a grin, "Try to limit your theatrical urges to daylight hours from now on. I'm going to try to get another hour's sleep so I don't spend Dr. Lingard's whole visit yawning at him." He pulled the door closed and shuffled back to his bedroom.

Not a bad idea, Dad, I thought. I told Elliott to wake me at 8:15 and I climbed back in bed. With "Anything You Can Do, I Can Do Better" playing in my head over and over, I fell into a deep sleep. No flashbacks. No nightmares.

Chapter 48

Dad had arranged for Elliott to watch out for Dr. Lingard, so we could give him our version of a Red Carpet welcome. As the doctor climbed out of his car, a bright green pathway took shape, leading from his car right to the main gate. As he approached the gate, it swung open and Elliott intoned with utmost courtesy, "WELCOME, DOCTOR! YOUR VISIT IS HIGHLY REGARDED BY US ALL! PLEASE PROCEED AHEAD ALONG THE PATH. THE LIGHTING WILL DIRECT YOU."

Since I had told Dad I'd be happy to meet Dr. Lingard and get him to the lab, I met our honored guest at the front door. It was 9:55.

"Daniel!" he said, reaching out to shake my hand. "I was hoping you'd be joining us."

"Thanks, doctor. I didn't want to butt in…"

"No butting at all," he said, gathering me to him with one arm. "Where are we headed?"

We followed the rabbit warren of hallways that led to Dad's personal lab, arriving on the dot of ten.

"Come in, come in!" Dad called to us from across the large laboratory. "I am so glad you are finally getting to see what we do here!" He came toward us along the marble counter to shake hands.

Over the next ninety minutes, Dad gave Dr. Lingard what he called "A Cook's Tour" of his lab and the two adjacent ones, where most of the current projects in DNA research were taking place. We weren't in danger of disturbing any experiments, although there were definitely a lot of petri dishes in multi-shelved refrigeration units scattered throughout the labs, so something was obviously in progress. Dr. Lingard asked Dad lots of questions – some Dad answered and some he sidestepped – but, all in all, the two most important men in my life seemed to be getting along "swimmingly."

I knew that Dad would save the GAR for the last stop on our tour, as he always called it his *piéce de resistance,* so it had to be the climax of the morning. Dr. Lingard looked puzzled as Dad led him up to the unit and flung his arms out in a "Ta-da!" gesture.

"What is this?" the doctor asked.

"This, my friend, is the Genetic Alteration Room, affectionately called the GAR. It's where a lot of the magic happens!"

"Is this where you create dino hybrids?" the doctor asked.

"Something like that," Dad said. "Mostly, we alter the genomes people were born with to enhance their hybrid lives. It's a little like finding a DNA marker for an inherited disease and switching it out for a marker that inhibits that disease from developing. Scientists working exclusively in human disease research have been doing this for years, as I'm sure you know."

"Yes, of course," the doctor said. "But what's this little box? It looks like something you'd put your hand in at a dance club to show you had been 'stamped.'"

Dad laughed. "Well, you're almost right," he said. "If you put your hand in this box, it can analyze your current DNA profile. Want to try it? It's painless!"

"OK, I guess," Dr. Lingard said, but I saw a strange look in his eye… Was it fear?

Nevertheless, he slipped his hand into the box, triggering a series of buzzes and beeps.

"Hold still for thirty seconds," Dad instructed. Dr. Lingard did as he was told, but I noticed that he was getting flushed and his breathing was getting faster and faster.

"Are you all right, doctor?" I asked, concerned.

"Yes," he said, "but I have a feeling I'm about to learn the answer to a mystery I have wondered about for most of my life…"

Just then the box dinged and printed out its report of Dr. Lingard's DNA profile. The doctor pulled his hand out of the box, turning it over and over, examining it and wiggling his fingers, as I grabbed the report. We all leaned together to read it, and each of us – at the same instant – zeroed in on one VERY *un-human* genome that was listed about two-thirds of the way down the "recipe."

"OMG… You're a dino hybrid, doctor!" I shrieked. "A *Pachyrinosaurus!* Why didn't you tell me?"

The doctor looked away. Several long seconds went by before he said, quietly, "Because until this moment, I didn't really want to believe it… not for sure, anyway."

When Dad and I looked at him skeptically, he went on to explain.

"My parents were always very bigoted against anybody who was not 'pure' ethnically. I'm sure they knew that my sister and I were dino hybrids – there have to have been signs as we grew — but having 'impure' kids would not have been acceptable to them. So I think that any time any hints of our dino traits started showing up, our parents must have punished us severely. It was pure action-reaction. I'm sure that it didn't take long for us to learn NOT to be our true selves. Unfortunately, I think that learning to deny our dino genome probably cost my best friend her life."

"What?!" Dad cried. "How?"

Dr. Lingard stared off to the left, recalling what was obviously a long-repressed, painful memory. "It was the summer I turned 14. Sally and I were walking home after seeing a movie. It was **Star Wars**, and we both loved it, so we were talking about our favorite scenes – not paying attention to anything, really. We didn't know that a *Suchomimus* from the uptown zoo had broken out and was roaming around town. Before the police found it, it found us." He teared up and reached for his handkerchief, dabbing at his eyes as he continued his story.

"When it attacked, I tried to morph into my dino form to defend us, but I had been brainwashed for so long that morphing was WRONG that I couldn't remember how to do it at first. I was only about a third of the way to a – What was it? – Oh, a *Pachyrinosaurus,* that's right – and I tried so hard, but the *Suchomimus* wounded Sally terribly. It ran off right after that, but Sally bled to death with me by her side. I kept telling her that the ambulance was on the way and that everything was going to be ok, but she just stared up at the sky — like she was watching a bird," he said in a whisper.

Dad and I stared at him, not knowing what to say.

"That was 24 years ago," he said. "And I have tried to block details of that memory ever since. Most of the time, I forget that I was trying to morph – or that I even had that ability. I just see us as two kids attacked by a large animal while walking home from a movie. But some things won't let me forget," he said, untucking and unbuttoning his shirt to expose his chest, which was crisscrossed with ugly scars. "I have these to make me remember. But Sally didn't get the chance to worry about memories," he said, with tears filling his eyes.

"Wow, I- I'm so sorry," I said, and Dad stepped forward to put an arm around the doctor.

Dr. Lingard smiled and shook his head. "It's all right. It happened a long time ago," he said, looking up with a sort of smile through his tears. "At least, now I know what dino hybrid I am and I can own it. No one can make me feel 'impure' ever again. What's more, I have something in common with you, Daniel – and with your wonderful Team. If you ever think you might need an aging *Pachyrinosaurus* on the Team, give me a call. Of course, I might be a little rusty…"

"Dr. Lingard, Team Triassic would be honored to have you," I said, and I meant it. I had always felt an unusual connection with him. Didn't I always think we had something special in common, some extraordinary link? Who would have thought it might have come from a dino hybrid connection?

What an unbelievable morning! I thought, waving to Dr. Lingard as he drove away toward town.

I wanted to check in on the kids at the hospital, so Mom and Sebastian picked me up just before noon outside the front gate. As soon as the car came to a stop, Sebastian jumped out of the front and climbed into the backseat so I could ride next to Mom. As we drove off, Sebastian leaned forward behind my right ear and tapped me on the shoulder. There was obviously something he needed to say that was apparently top-of-mind for him.

I turned a bit toward him and he leaned next to my ear. "Look," he whispered, "I'm sorry you saw me explode at the hospital. I never yelled at my father like that before," he said, glancing over at Mom to see if she was listening. But Mom is pretty savvy about pretending not to hear things like this, so she appeared to be concentrating on traffic, hearing nothing from Sebastian.

"You already apologized yesterday," I said, quietly, over my shoulder. "There's no need for another apology."

"I know," he persisted, "but I yelled at you and I know you were just trying to keep things from escalating," he said.

"Yeah, I was. We were in a crowded hospital ER, after all!" I said, in a stage-whisper. I stopped for a moment, trying to decide if I wanted to ask what had been bothering me since yesterday. Opting to "dive in," I turned around and asked Sebastian in a normal (aggravated) tone of voice, "If you don't mind me asking, why *did* you explode on your father like that?"

Mom glanced at me under furrowed brows, then returned to her "I hear nothing!" pretense.

Sebastian sighed and leaned back in his seat. I pushed down the headrest so I could maintain eye-contact with him, as he explained.

"Well, ever since he got back from deployment and became a security guard, he's been treating Xander and me like he's a general and we're his soldiers in Boot Camp. He tells us to do all sorts of things – most of them just to make us follow orders, I think — and he gets mad at us if we do anything slightly 'wrong.' Like loading the dishwasher… He wants the plates facing right but Mom always faced them left, so that's how we learned it. Does it really make a difference how they face? Well, it does to our Dad! Anytime we forget the right-left rule, we get a long lecture and he punishes us by making us wash dishes by hand for the next three days!"

I shook my head, feeling sorry for him and his brother. But Sebastian wasn't done.

"And folding towels is another example: We fold them the way Mom does, but he likes them to look rolled up. Anytime he finds folded towels in the linen closet, he throws them in the tub and turns on water so they get soaked and heavy. Then it's our job to get them to the laundry room without dripping water on the floor." He stopped and sighed. "I know they don't sound like very important things, but every day it's more orders, more lectures, new punishments. We feel like we have to tiptoe around the house when he's there to try to avoid him."

I just let him get it all off his chest. Mom kept staring straight ahead, pretending not to hear anything as she "concentrated on driving." I thought he had wound down, so I said, "Do you spend much time at your grandma's?"

He ignored my question, sitting up straight and almost exploding. "He also disrespected the hospital staff and YOU!" he almost shouted. "That was just too much!" He sank back into his seat, clenching his teeth, his hands closing into fists.

I nodded my head in understanding. "I see," I said sincerely. "I'm sorry that's it's been hard for you and Xander back home, especially without your mom."

Then it occurred to me that with Xander in the hospital for who-knows-how-long, Mr. Montgomery would pile all his bullying onto

Sebastian, so things could be worse… especially after Sebastian lashed out physically at his dad in the ER. Mr. Montgomery was a very fit 250 pounds, I'd estimate, so he could really hurt Sebastian.

"Grandma always says we can come to her house anytime, but they really don't have much room. Xander and I have to share a pretty old futon in the family room, which is where Grandpa often sleeps in his recliner, so it's not an ideal setup for any of us… although it's better than being in our house with Dad. Whenever I'm not at school, if he's home… I don't want to sound like a baby, but… I'm scared," he confessed in a whisper.

Mom suddenly gave up her pretense of not listening. She turned slightly toward Sebastian and said, "Sebastian, you are welcome to stay at our house for as long as you want. Our larger guest room is all yours. This evening we can just go get the rest of your clothes and whatever you need to be comfortable."

When Sebastian looked like he was going to protest, she said over her shoulder, "Not another word! Dinner is at 6:30." She nodded once and turned back to her driving.

"Thanks, Mrs. Robertson," Sebastian said. "I won't make you regret this." He wiped his eyes with his sleeve.

"Yeah, thanks, Mom," I said, reaching over to squeeze her free hand.

A couple of minutes of silence later, we drove up to the Guest Entrance of Centennial Hills Hospital and Sebastian and I got out. We said our thanks and waved goodbye to Mom and walked inside to see what this new day had in store for us.

Chapter 50

There was good news waiting for me at the Hospital Reception Desk. Dr. Lingard had left a message giving me an update on the general status of patients who came to Centennial Hills from the dino attack yesterday. It was written on two of those pink "While You Were Out" notes.

The first note concerned kids I had spent time with yesterday:

Nick Williamson – discharged

Aurora Brewer — discharged

Xander Montgomery – post-op recovery in room 519

Tucker Gilbert — post-op recovery in room 519

William Steinmetz — medical recovery in room 617

The second note listed twelve names of kids I didn't know, but I was happy to see the word "discharged" after each of their names.

I showed the notes to Sebastian, who said, "That's great news! Let's go tell Xander."

It was lunchtime for fifth-floor patients when we arrived. When we looked in the door, both Xander and Tucker were sitting up in their beds, poking at different colors and consistencies of hospital mush in their sectioned plastic trays, tentatively tasting one glob after the other, but not appearing to be finding anything very appetizing. We stood by the door, observing them. They hadn't noticed us yet.

"Did you try the orange stuff yet?" Tucker asked Xander. "Is it sweet potatoes or carrots... or something else?"

Xander tasted a little orange on the tip of his spoon. "I have no idea," he said. "It tastes like kindergarten paste to me."

When both Sebastian and I cracked up at that, Tucker and Xander finally noticed us. Tucker's eyes almost popped out of his head when he caught sight of Sebastian.

"Hey, guys… How long have you been standing there?" Xander asked.

"Just since your Orange Glob Analysis," Sebastian answered. Walking over to Tucker's bed, he said, "By the way, I'm Sebastian. I've seen you around Centennial, I think."

"Oh, yeah! For a second, I thought I was seeing double… and I don't need anything *else* wrong with me! And yeah, I guess I did know Xander's a twin."

We dragged two chairs to the center of the room, facing the patients in their beds so we could talk together easily. Both of them seemed to be in good spirits, but that might have been partially thanks to the two bags of Golden Relief hanging from their IVs. After about thirty minutes, I left Sebastian with his brother and Tucker and headed up to my old room to see William.

When I opened the door of room 617, I could see that the bed was empty and I felt a sudden coldness in my chest. Dr. Lingard's note had said William was "recovering," but…

Then Joseph was standing there, all aglow off to my left. His kind smile warmed my heart and I felt immediately calm.

"Daniel, you appear stressed. How can I help?"

"What happened to William?" I asked fearfully. "Did he… Is he…?"

Joseph smiled kindly. "No, no… He has a concussion, so he's downstairs undergoing an MRI. It's just to make sure there's no bleeding in his brain." When I looked scared, he quickly went on, "Doctors don't think there is, Daniel. This is just to make sure. Please don't worry."

A light tap on the door was Joseph's signal to disappear, I guess. Where he had been standing there was now just a lingering glow.

"Come in," I called.

The door opened and Evelyn stepped into the room, carrying a pile of linens.

Seeing me, she smiled widely and said, "Oh, hi, Daniel. I'm glad I ran into you. Dad said at lunch that he was going to look for you. I think he has some news about the mother of one of your friends."

"Xander's mother?" I asked, hoping.

"Gee, I don't know," she said. "He was conferring with Dr. Esterbrook about her – if that helps."

"It sure does!" I said, excitedly. "Thanks, Evelyn. I'll holo your dad and see where we can meet."

We said our goodbyes and "See ya laters" and I walked into the hall, tapping in a holo-text.

DANIEL Dr. Lingard, Evelyn says you have news about Mrs. Montgomery. Can we meet somewhere?

LINGARD Your timing is perfect. I'm in Xander and Tucker's room. Come on down!

Taking the stairs down by twos, I got to room 519 in less than two minutes. I courtesy-tapped on the door as I opened it, finding Dr. Lingard and a woman I didn't know standing by Xander's bed. Sebastian was on the other side of the bed, and all four of them turned to me as I entered.

"Oh, good, Daniel, you're here. Xander and Sebastian asked us to tell you about an idea we have come up with. By the way," he said, remembering his manners, "This is Dr. Esterbrook, who is treating Mrs. Montgomery."

The very pretty blonde woman who didn't look old enough to be a doctor walked to me and we shook hands.

"So you're the 'Daniel' I've been hearing so much about," she said. "I am pleased to finally meet you!"

"Pleased to meet you, too," I said, as I wondered who had been telling Dr. Esterbrook about me. I was hoping she hadn't gotten her impression of me from that original TV interview...

Sebastian stepped over to the other side of the room, asked Tucker if it was ok and then returned to Xander's side with Tucker's two chairs. We all sat down, two on either side of Xander's bed.

Dr. Lingard said, "Lily... er, Dr. Esterbrook has proposed something – that I agree is worth trying – to help bring Mrs. Montgomery out of her prolonged dissociative state. It is an aggressive procedure, so we wanted both Xander and Sebastian to weigh in. Lily?"

"Yes," Dr. Esterbrook said, taking up the conversation, "It is aggressive, to be sure, but everything else we have tried with your mother has had absolutely no effect – for years. Sometimes thinking 'out of the box' in medicine can have a very positive result. I think this may be one of those times."

Xander said, "Doctor, please tell Daniel what you told us. I want to hear what he thinks."

"Absolutely," Dr. Esterbrook said. "Daniel, as you know, Mrs. Montgomery's current condition is a sort of comatose state that resulted from the attack she and Xander suffered nearly five years ago. Although her eyes are open most days, she is completely cut off from almost everything. She does not respond to speech or touch. Her only normal response is when she is fed. She cannot feed herself, but she takes food from the spoon held by the nurse or nurse's assistant and chews and swallows normally. Other than that, she is in her own very dark place."

"That's so sad," I said.

"Yes, it is," Dr. Esterbrook said. "Mrs. Montgomery has *no* 'quality of life.' And that's the main reason we" – she gestured toward Dr. Lingard – "we feel this is worth trying."

Xander broke in. "What they want to do, Daniel, is bring Mom in here. They think that maybe seeing me in a hospital bed – wrecked again, like before – might trigger her Mama Bear instinct and bring her out of her trance. She hasn't seen me injured like this since that day we were attacked. Dr. Esterbrook says that when I've visited her over the years, she doesn't see me as Xander. I'm a stranger to her."

"Me, too," Sebastian said. "Both of us look different from the way she probably remembers us – if she has any memory of us at all, that is," he said, sadly.

A sudden thought popped into my head. "What does *Mr.* Montgomery have to say about this idea? Doesn't he have to approve his wife's treatment?" I asked, quietly.

The doctors looked at each other, then at the two boys. There was a delay, then Dr. Lingard took a deep breath and spoke.

"Two years ago Mr. Montgomery signed legal papers that removed him from any responsibility for his wife's care," he said. "Medical decisions are now the province of Mrs. Montgomery's medical staff, headed by Dr. Esterbrook."

I just shook my head. How could any husband do such a thing?

"I say let's do it," Sebastian said.

"Yes, I agree," Xander said. "It just might work. Nothing else has."

I didn't say anything – I felt that it wasn't my place to "weigh in" – but the proposed procedure sounded reasonable to me.

Plans were made to bring Mrs. Montgomery to Xander's room the next afternoon – "her most lucid time" – and both Dr. Esterbrook and Dr. Lingard would be there, along with two orderlies (for transport and in case things didn't go well). Tucker would be out of the room for a scheduled procedure, so the Montgomery family would have privacy.

"You need to be here, too, Daniel," Xander said. "You're like part of our family."

I was so touched that I was afraid I'd choke up, so I looked down, pretending a holo-text had just come in. Gesturing to the holo and pointing out the door, I did a quick mime routine to say I had to leave and I got out of there before my emotions could overtake me. I jogged to the elevator, pressed DOWN and was relieved when it arrived empty.

Chapter 52

My holo actually did suddenly buzz in my pocket as I stepped out of the elevator in the ER. Nick's face greeted me with his usual "Hey, Team!" He was sending out a Direct Message – not through Elliott (unusual) – to all of us, and he sounded pretty excited.

NICK Everybody, please stop whatever you're doing and make your way to Headquarters by 4 o'clock. I have something to share with everyone, something you'll want to see! Meet in the large conference room.

The general message faded and a private message to me popped up:

NICK Daniel, please bring our new recruits along with you, if they are available. I know about Sebastian and Aurora – If there are others, bring them, too.

I holo-texted him "OK" and started trying to figure out what he had up his sleeve. I holoed Aurora about Nick's "invitation," telling her that I'd pick her up (literally) at her house in thirty minutes. Then I holoed Sebastian to meet me at the hospital Guest Entrance at 3:30. On the way to Aurora's, I morphed to 25% so there would be room for both of them to ride and we'd get to Lone Mountain quickly. I was still trying to figure out Nick's "secret" at 3:40 when I de-morphed at the entrance gate and Sebastian and Aurora jumped off.

Nick must have forewarned Elliott that we would be admitting guests, because he didn't put Sebastian and Aurora through his usual Stranger

Interrogation. All he said as he swung the gate open was, "WELCOME, DANIEL AND DANIEL'S GUESTS."

We made our way to the large conference room, where Nick, Johnny, Kayla, Juli, Timeer, Lynnelle, Matthew and Michael were already seated around the table. Andy and Angel were right behind us, and they quickly took their places.

Before I had a chance to introduce Sebastian, Timeer stood up and applauded.

"Welcome back, Xander!" he said, looking at Sebastian.

Matthew laughed and said, "Applause is great, Timeer, but that's not Xander. Xander's still in the hospital. This is his twin, Sebastian."

"Yes, Sebastian is interested in joining his brother on the Team," I said. "And this is Aurora. She'll be coming on-board, too." Everybody reached across the table to take turns shaking hands with Sebastian and Aurora, murmuring "Welcome," "Great to have you," etc.

Then Juli stood up suddenly. "Xander isn't a dino, right?" she asked, looking at Sebastian. "So you're not one, either... right?"

"Right," he said, almost apologetically.

"Hooray!" Juli shouted. "One more for our side!"

Everybody was laughing their heads off as the three of us took our seats across from Nick. He looked around the table, mentally taking a head-count, then he stood, signaling the meeting was starting. We all quieted down immediately and turned our full attention to Nick. He started off with a very serious tone.

"Thanks to all of you for coming on short notice," he said. "Our Team has been put to the test this week and – in most instances – our months of hard training paid off. There is little doubt that the death and destruction at Centennial High would have been much, much worse if we had not been trained and ready to tackle a new manmade monster dinosaur. And I have complete faith that if the second dino monster had survived to participate in the attack, our Team would have been up to the challenge. Congratulations and thanks, everyone!" He led a round of applause that began uncertainly (We *were* applauding ourselves, after all!), but grew to include "Yeahs!" and whoops and all sorts of happy hollering.

When we quieted again, Nick went on. "So... I think it is perfectly appropriate today for us to have a little fun. And what better way to do that than to take a look at some rehearsal holos from 'Annie Get Your Gun,' the musical that Kayla and Juli will be performing in next week at the Spring Valley Little Theater." He pointed his holo at the wall-screen and the early Act I scene with Annie and her siblings came on. Juli on screen looked so happy as she said her pre-song lines, and Juli in the conference room looked even happier. Kayla just leaned back in her chair, enjoying the moment.

As the kids on screen broke into "Doin' What Comes Natur'lly," everybody started bopping to the beat and clapping in rhythm, laughing at the clever lyrics and the silly choreography. I, of course, followed every word in my head, since I had practiced it. When the song ended, wild applause filled the room. Juli looked about ready to cry from joy.

The scene changed and there was Kayla as Annie with her male co-star Brad Simpson as Frank Butler, facing each other with grim faces, hands on hips, as they began my favorite song from that play, "Anything You Can Do, I Can Do Better!" Again, the words were right in my head as Kayla and Brad fought it out musically. They were fabulous!

"Bravo!" I shouted when the song ended and the wild applause started again. "Bravo!"

I hoped I sounded sincere and happy, but the truth is that I had found myself getting more and more depressed with every chorus. I knew every word, of course, especially after my early-morning practice session in my bedroom, so I could have sung along easily. The fact was, though, that Nick's afternoon of fun for the Team was having a negative effect on me. Why? Because it made me realize just how much I miss acting! Playing parts for the wall screen in my bedroom was just not going to be enough, I decided right then and there. While the rest of the Team was whooping and hollering over our two Teammates' performances, I was making a life decision: I could not, would not, give up the Theater! And who knows… Maybe Team Triassic and Drama COULD co-exist in my life. I hoped so!

I brought my attention back to the here-and-now when Nick announced that he had another surprise for all of us. When the Team quieted enough for him to be heard, he pulled a bunch of tickets out of his pocket and announced, "I have tickets here for the three nights of the "Annie Get Your Gun" performances, enough for each of you and your families. For those of you who are scheduled for the evening shift next week, please take tickets for one of your nights off. I'm hoping that we can fill a couple of rows in the theater at least for each performance, so we can make lots of noise to support Kayla and Juli."

He spread the tickets on the table and we all reached for the night we preferred. I held up five Friday tickets for Andy to see, and he nodded, so the Robertsons and their lodger twin would be in the audience Friday night. *I might even go Saturday, too,* I thought to myself, looking to see if a Saturday ticket was left. Too bad for me, every ticket had been claimed. *Oh well, there's always buying a ticket at the door,* I figured. And who knows? Maybe someday the Team will be grabbing for tickets to one of MY performances!

As we made our way toward the door, I pulled Juli aside and asked her to show Sebastian and Aurora around the areas where "non-dinos" did their work.

"I think they'll be pretty impressed with the operation of the gym floor configurations," I told her.

After everybody else had left, I went up to Nick, put my arm around him and said, "Thanks, Bro. What you did today is what we all needed. You are a natural leader! What would we do without you?"

Without a word, Nick pulled away from my loose hold and made a big deal of gathering up papers and folders off his desk, keeping his head down the whole time. When he had a good-sized pile, he mumbled something about needing to get them to Angel for some reason and he scurried out of the room.

Now, what was THAT all about? I asked myself.

Two o'clock the next afternoon couldn't come fast enough for me. I was so eager to see how the "out-of-the-box" procedure with Mrs. Montgomery would go! I just hoped and prayed it would be one of those Medical Miracles you see on *Lifetime TV.*

I was waiting on the bench outside room 519 at 1:45 when Sebastian came out of the elevator. He walked over to me and I made room on the bench.

The door to 519 opened and Dr. Lingard welcomed us inside, where Xander was sitting up in his bed, but a little slouched. Instead of a hospital gown, he was wearing his own PJs and his hair was combed forward to give him the appearance of bangs. He looked lots younger.

Sebastian shook hands with Dr. Lingard, mumbling something that sounded like "Thank you for this," and he and I waved at Xander as we walked around to the other side of his bed. Sebastian put his chair a little behind Dr. Lingard and me. When we were all in place, the doctor spoke into his holo.

"They'll be here in a couple of minutes," he told us.

We were all edgy, I guess, so nobody said much of anything while we waited. Soon we could hear the elevator open and close and less than a minute later a light tap on the door let us know the rest of our group had arrived.

One orderly pushed open the door so the other one could maneuver Mrs. Montgomery's wheelchair into the room. Dr. Esterbrook followed, and all of them crossed the room to the near side of Xander's bed. The wheelchair orderly fixed the brakes, adjusted Mrs. Montgomery's lap blanket and stepped behind the chair. Mrs. Montgomery stared straight ahead, expressionless.

Dr. Esterbrook walked toward the front of the wheelchair, taking care not to step between her patient and the boy in the bed. She got down on one knee and spoke softly.

"Maria, I'm Dr. Esterbrook. I have been caring for you. Today I have brought you to visit someone… someone you know. Maria, do you see the boy in the bed?"

Mrs. Montgomery kept staring ahead.

Dr. Esterbrook reached up and put her hand under her patient's chin and used gentle pressure to turn Mrs. Montgomery's head more toward Xander. The patient's face remained blank.

I hadn't noticed it before, but a kid's alarm clock now sat on Xander's bedside chest. It must have been prearranged, because it suddenly emitted a loud "Vroom vroom!" car revving sound that went on and on until Xander reached over and slammed his hand down on it.

That must have been Sebastian's cue. He growled at his brother, "Get up, Lazy!"

Mrs. Montgomery's eyes fluttered.

Nobody knew what to do next. Then – out of the blue — Xander did what he had probably done a hundred times as a kid. He looked over at Sebastian and whined in a high-pitched voice, "Bro, leave me alone. I'm not going to school today!"

Something flashed across his mother's face. Was it recognition? A sudden flicker of memory?

Dr. Esterbrook motioned to Xander to "keep it up."

Xander turned his back on his brother – which made him face his mother – and put his hands over his ears. "Bro, I can't hear you," he said in a dramatically tired voice. "Let me sleep!"

Another flash crossed Mrs. Montgomery's face, and this time her hand came up from her lap, her pointer finger extended and shaking.

Xander and Sebastian both actually laughed.

"That's her 'Listen to me!' gesture," Sebastian whispered to me, excited.

"Whenever we whined about anything, that shaky pointer finger came up and we knew we were in trouble!" He grinned as he explained it to us all.

"Go ahead," Dr. Esterbrook urged Xander quietly. "This is real progress. Keep helping her to remember."

Xander pulled his pillow on top of his head. Sebastian looked over his shoulder, as if speaking to someone in another room, and called "Mom, I can't get Xander up and I need to get in the shower. Can you come and help?"

Xander peered out from under his pillow.

During the next sixty seconds, all of us in that room saw a miracle happen. Mrs. Montgomery shook her head, like she was trying to loosen something inside. She blinked her eyes about a dozen times then rubbed her nose very slowly with the back of her hand and took a long, deep breath.

Then her eyes opened wide. They sparkled as she looked at Xander in his bed and said, in very raspy but firm voice, "No, you may *not* stay in bed. You are going to school today, just like every day. GET UP!"

Dr. Lingard's chin dropped and his eyes bugged out of his head. Xander and Sebastian just stared at each other. Dr. Esterbrook smiled and shook her head in amazement. I almost fainted.

Dr. Esterbrook picked up a water cup with a sippy-straw from the bedside table and held it for her patient.

Mrs. Montgomery took several long swallows, then looked up at the doctor and around the room. Dr. Esterbrook took hold of both of her patient's hands, gently rubbing her fingers. Looking into Mrs. Montgomery's eyes, she spoke softly.

"Maria, I'm Dr. Esterbrook and I've been taking care of you. We are so happy that you are back with us. Your sons have missed you."

"Since they *went to bed?*" Maria asked, appearing suddenly confused at her surroundings. She looked around the room. "Where are we? Is this a hospital? I thought we were home. Is Xander sick?"

Dr. Esterbrook leaned down to release the wheelchair brakes and swung the chair around slowly to face the door as she said, "Yes, Maria, this is a hospital. But you're not to worry. Xander got a little banged up but he's going to be ok. You must be hungry. Why don't we go down to the cafeteria and I can fill you in while we have a little breakfast?"

Still confused, but willing to go along, Maria nodded. When she sat up a little straighter in the normally-reclined wheelchair, Dr. Esterbrook quickly adjusted the angle of the seatback for a more upright position.

The orderly opened the door and the doctor wheeled her patient out. All of us left in room 519 were still looking at each other, speechless, as we heard the elevator door open and close.

Chapter 54

Dear Diary,

This week was one for my memory book, to be sure! Yesterday afternoon Nick called a mandatory meeting, and since we hadn't had one of them for quite a while, we were all a little nervous as we gathered in the conference room. But the meeting turned out to be FUN! I guess as a Leader, Nick felt that we all needed a diversion after all the horror associated with the dino attack AND he probably wanted to give some "press" to Kayla and Juli and their play. So he showed us holos of the girls doing two of their "Annie Get Your Gun" songs in rehearsal. Both girls were fabulous! Then he gave us play tickets FOR OUR WHOLE FAMILIES!

And this afternoon we learned that a true miracle happened at Centennial Hills Hospital. No, it wasn't with one of the kids – which would have been great, too – but this was Xander's mother. SHE WOKE UP AFTER NEARLY FIVE YEARS! I don't know all the details, but I understand it was the idea of Daniel's doctor, Dr. Lingard, and Mrs. Montgomery's doctor to try a new therapy... and IT WORKED! Everybody is hoping she will stay well so she can go home soon. I am praying for her!

One thing that happened late today has me a little worried, though. I went in to Nick's office to say goodbye for the day and I caught him packing up a lot of his personal things and I thought he was crying. When he saw me, he quickly wiped his face with his sleeve, said, "Allergies" – which I didn't believe for a minute – and he asked me not to say anything to anybody about what I saw. He said he was "dealing with a family situation," which didn't make sense to me, but I could tell he wasn't about to say more, so I said "Bye" and left. What's going on???

Lynnelle

A lot happened in the next couple of days.

Dr. Lingard filled me in on what was happening when I called him for an update two days after "the miracle." He said he and Dr. Esterbrook were continually monitoring Mrs. Montgomery's progress, carefully explaining to her why she was in a hospital herself and what her continuing therapy would be, now that her dissociative state had faded. Everyone knew that she would probably continue to suffer residual effects from her prolonged coma, but the doctors are hoping they can put conditions in place that will minimize her episodes and let her enjoy life again.

Until they feel comfortable discharging Mrs. Montgomery to home care, the doctors have proposed making her hospital room look a little more like her home. Sebastian brought in about a dozen framed family photos and other mementos that the nurses arranged around the room.

Dr. Lingard said Dr. Esterbrook wanted to give Mrs. Montgomery even more of "a touch of normalcy," and all of her long-time nurses had seized the opportunity eagerly. They have even been bringing in some homemade dishes that they had learned were their patient's favorites.

"They felt so helpless with Maria's illness for years, Daniel," he said to me. "Now they can help Mrs. Montgomery to come back to her family fully."

I was so happy to hear that. But Dr. Lingard's next news was even better...

"Daniel," he said, "I've been speaking with your Mom and Dad today about an idea I have and they are on-board. Want to hear about it?"

"Sure, doctor! What's up?" I asked eagerly.

"Well, I understand that your mother is already 'spoiling' Sebastian at your house, and with Mrs. Montgomery still at the hospital for a while…"

I interrupted, shouting "*Of course*, Sebastian can keep staying with us!"

"But I wasn't finished, Daniel. Hold on a minute!" he said, in a bit of a huff.

"Oh, sorry, Dr. Lingard," I said, embarrassed. "Go on, please."

"As I started to say," he continued, "Your parents already have ONE twin staying with you, so I talked with your mother yesterday and we agreed. What's one more?"

When I gasped, he went on. "Xander can be discharged tomorrow, as long as he has a safe place to go. We can have Home Health nursing check on him once or twice every day as long as necessary – to change bandages, monitor his vitals, change IV fluids, etc. – but mostly, I'd say you and your brother can have yourselves two new roommates! What do you think?"

"What do I *think?!*" I repeated, completely out of breath. "I think you are the GREATEST DOCTOR IN THE WORLD… That's what I think, Dr. Lingard. Thank you, thank you thank you!"

Chapter 56

Xander arrived by ambulance on Wednesday, and Mom fussed about getting him settled, asking him if he was comfortable (about five times) and just generally being the perfect combination of Mom and Nurse. Dad and Andy had replaced the queen-sized bed in our larger guest room with two super-single beds, so our twin lodgers could share space the way they had always done. Andy installed a wall screen in the room giving the twins access to Elliott, and Dad even carried in a mini-fridge – like the ones Andy and I had — so Xander and Sebastian could always have bottled water, fresh fruit and juice available. (Mom always wanted us to "eat healthy," even when snacking.)

I was surprised that the IV set-up Xander arrived with didn't include the bag of Golden Relief that had been so necessary to his comfort level just a few days ago. When I asked about it, Xander explained.

"I'm healing really fast," he said. "As long as I don't move around too much, the new meds Dr. Lingard prescribed for me seem to be doing the trick." He held up a bottle of the largest capsules I think I ever saw.

"Are those for you or for someone running in the Kentucky Derby?" I asked, amazed.

"They're for me," he said, laughing – then suddenly stopping and holding his ribs.

"Spasm?" I asked.

Breathlessly, he gasped, "Ye-sss."

177

"So I guess The Comedy Channel is out for a while," I said with a wink.

He breathed shallowly and nodded. I took that as my signal to leave him alone to rest, so I patted his shoulder softly and waved goodbye.

"See you later, Bro," I said as I left the room and closed the door. I had a sparring match scheduled with Johnny in an hour, anyway, so I decided to head up the path to Lone Mountain on foot. The weather was a crisp 46 degrees and the smog wasn't bad at all… Just a perfect day for a stroll in Las Vegas!

About thirty minutes later, Elliott welcomed me and swung open the gate. It was cool the way we Team Triassic members no longer had to go through Security to get into the Lone Mountain complex. It made me feel special every time it happened!

As usual, Johnny was jazzed about our sparring match, so he was already positioned behind the Rio in the City Configuration and fully morphed when I got to the gym. I was pretty jazzed, too, because Johnny's eighteen-foot *Ostafrikasaurus* was a very worthy opponent to my *Regem Insuprabilus*, so I knew our match would be fun. I wanted to drop off my jacket before morphing, so I dashed along the gym perimeter to the office.

I was surprised to find the door to our office and the blinds both closed. This was very unusual. I hesitated a few seconds, trying to decide whether to KNOCK ON MY OWN OFFICE DOOR or just barge in. *It's my office, for heaven's sake,* I decided, and I thrust open the door.

Nick and Angel were sitting on the floor across the room from me, surrounded by piles of printed holo photos. They both jumped when they heard the door open and Nick whirled around, trying to push the piles of photos behind him.

"Daniel!" he cried. "What are you doing here? Don't you have a sparring scheduled?"

Angel sat silent, looking like a kid who just got caught with his hand in the cookie jar.

"What am I doing here?" I repeated, in my most "annoyed" voice. "I'm dropping off my jacket," I said, holding it up. "What are YOU doing here, sitting on the floor going through pictures?"

Angel jumped up, as Nick pushed the photo piles behind the corner file cabinet. They both had the guiltiest look on their faces that I think

I'd ever seen on anyone, but Nick tried to play it off with a casual hand gesture.

"Oh, it's nothing," he said. "Just going through some photos we might want to put on our website... or someplace. I guess we lost track of time. Sorry." He looked at his brother. "Angel, are you ready to head home?"

Angel nodded eagerly and kept his head ducked down as he scurried past me out the door.

"Uh, see you tomorrow, Daniel," Nick said with a sort of wave as he quickly followed his brother toward the exit.

I stood there in my office for a few minutes, trying to figure out what was going on, until Elliott holoed me that I was "2.5 MINUTES LATE" for my sparring match. I stepped into the gym and morphed, knowing that today's match would be different, since Johnny and I had not battled in the City Configuration before. Michael and Lynnelle were the Overseers this afternoon. Once they took their places, the buzzer sounded and the match was on!

The whole battle was just that... FUN. The two of us were evenly matched in so many ways that the match went back and forth, back and forth for all three periods. *Michael and Lynnelle have their work cut out for them this time,* I said to myself as Johnny and I de-morphed and gave each other a congratulatory hug.

I was still feeling the delight of a match well-fought when Lynnelle approached me with a worried look on her face. She pulled me aside and asked quietly, "What's going on with Nick and Angel?" When I just shrugged, she went on. "The other morning in our meeting Nick was so happy. Then later that day I think I caught him actually *crying* in your office! He told me that they're dealing with family problems and not to say anything. So I didn't. Do you know anything, Daniel?"

I had to confess that I didn't. "I'll try to talk to him and see what's going on," I told them. "Please don't worry."

But *I* was worried enough for all of us. What was up with Nick and Angel?

Chapter 57

I started sending holo messages – photo and text – to Nick later that day, but I never got through. At first, I thought he might be napping or that his holo was in another room (or both), but when he failed to answer after my ten tries, I came to the conclusion that he was avoiding me. Apparently, he wasn't in a mood for conversation.

I decided to leave him alone. *He'll come around eventually,* I figured.

Friday morning all the buzz at Headquarters was about Kayla and Juli's play. Matthew, Timeer and Aurora and their families had attended the Thursday Opening Night performance and they couldn't stop talking about how great it was. Kayla and Juli were all smiles, taking it all in.

Not usually one for handing out compliments, Matthew sounded shockingly over-the-top when he described Juli's performance as "spectacular" and announced that "Kayla stole the show!"

Timeer chimed in, too.

"My Dad usually hates musicals, but he went because the tickets were free. And he LOVED it! He even said he might try to get tickets for Saturday and take Gram!"

Aurora's parents were just as enthusiastic, she agreed. "But my parents love the theater, so I expected them to have a good time," she said. "What I *didn't* expect was their insistence since last night that *I* need to try out for the Little Theater's next production. I'm really not the 'theater type.'

The only reason I was in the Drama class that got attacked was because the Art History class I wanted was full."

"But… did YOU enjoy the play?" Kayla asked, lowering one eyebrow.

"Oh yes!" Aurora said, sincerely. "But I can't imagine – myself – being up there on stage and not fainting!"

"It's not so bad," Juli said. "Our first director back in Molasky told us that if we start feeling stage-fright coming on, 'Just picture the audience in their underwear. It will relieve your stress so you can enjoy playing your part.' I used to have to do that all the time," she said. "But the last few plays I was in, my audiences could remain fully-clothed!"

"That's good," Johnny joked, "because our tickets are for tonight and that theater can be a little drafty. It could be a little uncomfortable if I thought you were seeing me sitting there in my Jockey shorts."

Lynnelle turned bright red and Timeer gasped. The rest of us all decided suddenly that we had to be somewhere else and we scattered, leaving Johnny standing alone. He looked from one fleeing Team member to another.

"What? Wha-at did I thay?"

Chapter 58

After the rave reviews I heard from the Thursday play-goers, I was more eager than ever to see the performance with my family on Friday night. When I say "my family," you have to remember that our house was now home to four teenage boys. And that brought up a "situation."

Xander was still far from full recovery, but he had heard enough about Kayla and Juli's play to ask if there was any way for him to go along with us to the theater. He only needed his IV at night now, so that would not pose a problem; but would it endanger his recovery to ride in a car for twenty minutes each way and sit in a theater seat for two hours? We needed to ask Dr. Lingard.

> **XANDER** Doctor, would it be ok for me to go to the theater tonight? Kayla and Juli are in a play and I'd like to see it.

> **LINGARD** Xander, you are two days out of the hospital. I will not say NO, but I worry that going might set you back. Isn't there another alternative?

And that's when inspiration hit me. Elliott! Unlike film or videotape of the old days, Elliott's holos are so lifelike that you feel like you're actually there. If I could get special permission from the theater for Elliott to holo the performance, Xander could see the play the same way we would.

I holoed Dr. Lingard:

DANIEL I think we'll try to get the play director to let Elliott holo the performance for Xander. Kayla and Juli must have his number.

LINGARD No need. My wife was usually the director for Spring Valley Little Theater plays, but she couldn't do this one because of her due-date. We'll call Hector immediately and get permission.

I thanked Dr. Lingard and went to tell Xander about the arrangements. I think he was a little relieved how things turned out. He couldn't have been looking forward to what would inevitably have been a painful experience. After all, *laughing* caused pain spasms, and one thing I think there are a lot of are laughs in "Annie Get Your Gun." With the holo, Xander could watch as much of the play as he wanted at a time. Or he could wait a week or so...

At 7 p.m., the rest of us said goodbye to Xander and we headed to the theater in Mom's SUV. Of course, before we left, Mom had loaded Xander's bedside table with bowls of beef jerky, cut-up pineapple, chips and salsa and a plate of homemade cookies. When Xander protested, saying "We just had dinner!" Mom wouldn't hear of it.

"Young man," she said sternly, "You need to regain your strength! I expect you to eat every bit of this food. No excuses!"

Now, I could probably go on and on about how COMPLETELY, TOTALLY FABULOUS "Annie Get Your Gun" – and Kayla and Juli – were, but that could take up many paragraphs. Let's just say that I have never been prouder of my two friends from Molasky's Drama I class than I was that night! And I wasn't alone, either. The whole audience rose to its feet at the curtain-call and nobody stopped applauding, whooping and hollering until the curtain opened again to reveal the whole cast standing there, pretty overwhelmed by it all.

A man who was probably Hector walked partway down the aisle to catch the eye of the orchestra conductor, who shrugged and asked, "Which one?"

"Show Business – Finale," the maybe-Hector mouthed.

Well, I was hoping they'd do "Anything You Can Do" again, but I realized that the "No Business Like Show Business" number had everybody on stage, so it was the logical choice. What's more, it was apparently a song that nearly everybody in the audience knew, because we all sang along. It was wonderful!

Mom, Dad, Andy, Sebastian and I sang "There's No Business Like Show Business!" all the way home. Dad and Andy even added some harmony. It was so much fun!

First thing in the morning, I got up, showered quickly and grabbed two donuts out of the pantry. Mom was already in the car, waiting, so I ate the donuts on our way to Centennial Hills Hospital to check on Tucker and William, who were both still recovering there from the dino attack.

I rode up to the sixth floor to check in on William, but he wasn't in his room. A practical nurse passing me in the hall said, "He's downstairs in Radiology."

I had no better luck in room 519. The nurse making Tucker's bed said he was "downstairs having some procedure."

When she dropped me off, Mom had said she was doing some quick shopping at WalMart, so I was hoping I could catch her for a ride back home after my fruitless visit to the hospital. I sent a text:

DANIEL: R U still nearby? Need a ride home.

MOM: Just checking out. See you in 10

While I waited for my chauffeur, I tried Nick on the holo. No answer.

I was back home by nine. When I still hadn't gotten in touch with Nick by 10 o'clock, I decided to take matters into my own hands. I woke up Andy, who was NOT happy to be awake before noon on a Saturday, and asked him to drive me to Nick's.

"Ride a bike," he barked. "I think there are still two in the garage."

"There's not one whole bike there. Don't you remember you took our bikes apart to create a 'faster' model?"

"Oh yeah, I need to get to that. Can't Mom take you?"

"She took me to the hospital earlier, but then she went off again, more shopping."

"What about Dad?"

"He's up at Lone Mountain. C'mon, Andy, just take me. You can sleep all afternoon if you want."

He grumbled some more, then flung off his quilt and crawled out of bed.

"You'll owe me for this," he said as he pulled some clothes off one of his piles and dressed. Nothing matched, but I was not about to say anything.

"Let me brush my teeth at least," he said, and he was off to the bathroom. I went downstairs to wait.

A long ten minutes later – just when I was thinking he probably went back to bed – my sleepyhead brother came down the stairs jingling his car keys.

"Let's go!" he said with a "hurry-up" gesture, as though I was the one making HIM wait. I just shook my head in disbelief.

Chapter 60

With Andy driving, it took us only seven minutes to get to Nick's. Both Mom and Dad are "careful drivers" (Read: SLOW), so Andy's speed always seemed to me like I'm with a racecar driver. As we turned into the Williamsons' driveway, I was preparing to start breathing normally again when Andy screeched to a halt about six inches in front of the garage. At that very instant, the single-bay garage door started going up, revealing Angel and Nick standing there, side-by-side. That entire section of their three-car garage was filled with cardboard boxes of every size and shape imaginable.

Angel approached the driver's side, so Andy opened his window

"Hey," Angel said.

"Hey," Andy replied. "You're expecting us?"

"Kind-of," Angel said. "Nick knew your brother wouldn't take being ignored for very long. And we wanted to see both of you, actually."

I leaned across the seat. "Why both of us?" I asked.

Nick walked up to stand next to Angel. "We need to take you somewhere," he said. "It's important. Do you have some time?"

Andy looked at me under lowered brows. I knew he did NOT want to spend his Saturday doing anything that did not involve sleeping.

"Does it have to be today?" Andy asked in a sort of whiny voice.

"Well, actually, yes it does," Nick said.

Andy rolled his eyes, sighed deeply and then said, "Oh, all right. Get in. This better not take all day!"

Angel went back into the garage and picked up a shoebox-sized wooden crate, and he and Nick climbed in the back seat. Andy backed out of their driveway. "Where to?" he asked over his shoulder as he swung the car around ninety degrees, flinging us all first right, then left in our seats.

"Mount Charleston, please, driver!" Angel said, steadying himself.

"Where?" I asked, turning around to look at Nick. "Did he say 'Mount Charleston'?"

Nick ducked his head and said, "Yep" to his lap.

He didn't appear to be wanting to say anything else, so I just turned around in my seat.

Sensing the tension that threatened to consume the car, Andy said, "How about some music?" He flipped on his car holo, which entertained us with Classic Rock tunes for the forty-five minute ride to the forest entrance on Mount Charleston. No one spoke the whole way.

Chapter 61

When we all climbed out of the car, Andy and I just stood next to it, waiting for whatever was next.

"Remember this path?" Nick asked me, pointing to one that veered off to the left through the tall trees.

It was the path to their treehouse. "Yes, I remember, Nick. Are we showing Andy your treehouse? Is that what is so important… what *has* to be done today?" I asked, irritably.

"Actually, yes," Angel said, and he started down the path, the wood box under his arm.

We walked through the forest, winding in and out of pine clusters and deciduous varieties. Under normal circumstances, I would be enjoying the wonderful aromas and the peaceful quiet of the forest; but I was still annoyed that Nick had avoided me for over a day and then hijacked our Saturday for a trip to a treehouse.

Andy surprised me a little way in by leaning over and whispering, "Hey, this place is pretty awesome!"

I just shrugged and kept walking.

We were at a point where I thought we were getting close when we started noticing some smashed bushes and broken trees. The damage looked a little like what a tornado does, but it was more random, like something large animals would leave behind.

As we walked along, the destruction of trees and undergrowth increased.

"What happened here?" Angel asked in alarm. "Something has been up here destroying our forest!"

Nick took off running down the path, clearing away broken branches that obscured the trail as he ran.

We all picked up the pace to keep him in view.

He had just slipped out of sight around a thick stand of Quaking Aspens when we heard him wail, "OH NO!"

We rounded the aspens and saw Nick on his knees in front of a large pile of smashed two-by-fours, broken shingles, crushed steps and shattered plywood that had once been parts of a much-loved treehouse. All that remained intact was – strangely — the top four rungs of the rickety wooden ladder hanging from a broken section of the treehouse floor.

"What happened?" I cried. "Was there a tornado?"

"I don't know," Angel said, "but this is just a little too ironic for my taste."

"Ironic?" I asked. "How is it ironic?"

He was about to answer when Nick said, "Wait!"

Without another word, he pointed a shaky finger to a spot to the left of the pile. When Andy and I walked over to have a look, Andy suddenly wheeled around, banging into me.

"What are THEY?" he asked, pointing at depressions in the dirt that could be footprints.

I walked over to get a better look. "They're much too big to be human," I said, peering closer and pointing. "Whatever was here, it was barefoot. And there are divots here like the ones claws make. See?" I pulled out my holo and snapped a few shots.

While we were examining the footprints, Angel had walked around to the right side of the pile. He motioned us over, saying, "Guys, come over here. Have a look."

Nick led Andy and me around the rubble to where Angel stood. He gestured toward a flat piece of plywood that had a curved gouge in it, dead-center. All of us looked closely at this piece of plywood, the only one with anything recent cut into it, and then we all saw it:

"It looks like it was carved," Andy said, tracing the curved gash with a stick. "Somebody — or some THING — gouged a sort of Nike 'swoosh' on this piece of wood. Why?"

We all looked at each other and shrugged. A swoosh? No… Something was nagging at the back of my mind, but I couldn't bring it into focus. I looked at the other three, but no one seemed to have a good explanation.

"Anyway, it's all ironic," Angel said again.

This time I was going to get an answer from him. "Why ironic?" I insisted.

He and Nick looked at each other, and Angel said, "Nick, it's time." He walked over and picked up the wooden box. "Let's sit on the wood pile over there. It looks safe enough."

We each chose a spot and sat.

Nick gestured to Angel to begin. Clearing his throat, Angel started, a little hesitantly.

"We – Nick and I – wanted to bring you two up here today to give you something."

When Andy and I looked at him sideways under lowered brows, he hurried to rephrase.

"Well, it's not just something we can *hand* you. You see, Nick and I wanted to give you this…" He held out the wooden box to me – "and all this." He waved his arm to take in the whole clearing we were standing in. "The two go together."

"But it is all worthless now," Nick said, and his eyes glistened.

"What's in the box?" I asked.

"Open it," Angel said. "You both need to see what's inside."

I took the box, set it down on the ground between Andy and me and opened the lid. Inside was a pile of photos, some old Polaroids, some newer ones. As I started leafing through them, handing them one by one to Andy, I saw that they all had the same setting... here at the treehouse. A few old Polaroids pictured the treehouse high in the pine tree as it must have looked when Angel and Nick first discovered it ten years ago. It was already pretty weathered-looking, it had no ladder access and half of the floor had already fallen to the ground.

More recent photos showed the progress of the Williamson brothers' treehouse rebuilding project. In a few pictures, there was a makeshift ladder and rope contraption that was anchored precariously around a branch near the bottom of the treehouse – obviously the way the guys lifted both themselves and their building materials to repair the floor.

As we saw the treehouse that I remembered from my earlier visit taking shape in the photos, I began to realize just how important this place had been to Nick and Angel... for *years*.

Lingering over some of the photos taken of one brother by the other, as well as a few very recent "selfies," Andy and I could see pure happiness in their faces. They loved this place!

I was a little overwhelmed, so I was relieved when Andy spoke up. My big brother said the very words I was thinking: "Guys, this treehouse has been a true forest sanctuary for both of you. I am so very sorry it has been destroyed... after all your work!" Then he looked at me and nodded once. "No worries," he said with conviction. "We'll help you rebuild it, won't we, Dan?"

I was ready to agree heartily, but then stopped when I saw the way Angel and Nick looked at each other. It was apparent that they were wrestling with what to say to us. Then Angel cleared his throat.

"I said that this destruction of our treehouse is ironic, because it really is," he began. He looked sadly at his brother and continued. "We brought you up here today so we could give you our treehouse, since we won't be coming here anymore."

"*What?* Why not?" I asked, not "getting it."

Nick signed deeply. "We're leaving Las Vegas," he said in a whisper, his eyes lowered. Two tears dropped onto the ground at his feet

Andy and I looked at each other, then at Angel and Nick, in shock.

"You're LEAVING?!" I screamed, jumping up. "Leaving for WHERE? For HOW LONG?"

Now Nick was really crying. Between sobs and hiccups, he managed to say, "N-new Jer-jersey" in an almost childlike voice. Angel moved to put his arm around his brother.

"It's a permanent move," Angel said.

Right then I remembered all those packed boxes, the kitchen utensils ready for packing and a few comments that members of the Williamson family had made recently. At the time, the comments just seemed strange. Now they suddenly made sense. And Nick's weird behavior the last few days made sense, too.

"When? When are you moving?" I asked, confused. "Your house isn't even for sale!"

"Well, no... Mom and Dad accepted a full-price offer the day before it was to get multiple-listed. That was three weeks ago," Angel said. "We're moving on Monday."

I stood up, planted both feet and confronted Nick, leaning into his face.

"*THIS* MONDAY??! WHY DID YOU WAIT UNTIL NOW TO TELL ME?" I was bellowing and my words echoed through the forest. "YOUR FAMILY IS MOVING AWAY *TWO DAYS* FROM NOW? What if Andy and I hadn't been available today – or tomorrow... Were you just planning to LEAVE TOWN without telling us? I *thought* you were my best friend!"

I knew my tirade was out of control, but there was no way I could stop. I felt so… BETRAYED.

"WHAT ABOUT THE TEAM?!" I screamed, way beyond upset. "Do they know? Was all this just a secret from ME?"

Angel stood up, stepping between me and his brother. He put his hands out in a gesture of protection, I guess, but my breath kept coming in short, ugly gasps.

"No one knows," he said in a calm, even voice. "We didn't tell you before now because we both kept hoping the move would never happen."

"What?" I asked, a little skeptically. "You have a garage full of packed boxes and your parents have been making strange comments for weeks. Your house was sold three weeks ago. This move has been PLANNED FOR A LONG TIME! Don't try to tell me that moving NEXT MONDAY was a last-minute family decision!"

All this time, Andy had remained silent. Now he stood up and put his hands on my shoulders.

"Bro, listen to what they're telling you. I know you're upset, but look at them… They're both suffering. They have brought us here today to give us their most prized possession, the place where they made memories for more than TEN years, because their parents are moving them away. It has definitely not been Angel and Nick's decision. And I can see how – as kids not having a say in all of it – that they kept hoping things would change and the move would be canceled." He turned to Angel and asked, "Is that kind of what's going on here?"

Angel nodded. "It's Mom's career," he said. "A few months ago, Mom got a job offer from Clara Yost, her old college roommate, who has a really successful interior and set design business in Cape May, New Jersey. Clara has clients on Broadway, in Philadelphia and in Baltimore, so having her design studio in New Jersey is convenient for her and her clients. Besides, Clara loves everything Victorian, and that's what Cape May is known for, so that's where she wants to live."

He looked at Nick, eyebrows raised in question. Nick nodded, wiped a sleeve cross his face and took up the story.

"At first, Mom thought maybe she could telecommute – doing designs here in Vegas and sending them online," he said, "but a lot of Clara's follow-up business is done on-site, so telecommuting was out. We thought she was all ready to turn down the job, but then Clara told Mom she would 'sweeten the pot' by offering her a *full partnership* in the business at the end of one year. At that point, Mom and Dad had decided that Mom would go to New Jersey for the first year alone – to see how things worked out – and Dad, Angel and I would stay here."

Angel cut in. "We were so relieved… a lot could happen in one year, we figured."

But we could tell the story was not finished. "So what happened to that plan?" I asked.

Nick shook his head sadly. "Well, you know that Dad's a lawyer, right?"

Andy and I nodded.

Nick took in a deep breath and sounded pretty defeated as he continued their story.

"What you probably don't know is that Dad graduated from Rutgers and practiced law in New Jersey for two years out of law school, so he's admitted to the bar in New Jersey. Well, Clara had 'made some calls' to her friends in Trenton and before we knew it, Dad got a partner-track job offer from one of the state's top law firms. They want him to set up an office in South Jersey."

"So that was it," Andy said, resigned.

"Yep," Nick said, wiping his cheeks on his sleeve, standing up to face us.

Andy and I just stood there, neither of us knowing what to say.

Angel reached down, scooped up the photos and started putting them back in the box. He handed it to Andy. He said, "We waited until today to share our last treehouse visit and pass this special place on to you. Dad told us last weekend that the move was definitely on, but – to be completely honest – both of us still held out hope something would happen. We've both been not ourselves over this… Maybe you noticed?"

I nodded, as memories of Nick's "on-again, off-again" recent behavior and their mad-dash out of the office flashed through my mind.

"Yeah," I said, looking right at Nick. "There's NO WAY things have been 'normal' recently. I should have realized… I should have insisted that you talk to me."

"We probably wouldn't have been able to tell you, anyway," Nick said and Angel nodded.

"It's been hard enough today," he said.

"So THAT'S why you kept saying the destroyed treehouse was 'ironic!'" Andy said, with sudden understanding. "You were hoping to preserve your childhood memories of Las Vegas by leaving the treehouse to us. But now you see the place where you made all those memories is gone. There is a certain irony there, I guess. But look," he said, holding out the box to Nick, "your memories are here, intact in this box of photos – and in your memories, too."

I knew my brother was right. "Nobody – not even whoever or whatever destroyed this wonderful spot – can take your memories from you," I said to Nick and Angel. "And I'm sorry I went off on you before. I was just so upset and I didn't understand. Now I do." I reached out to pull Nick into a hug. Angel and Andy stepped up to join in.

"All better!" Andy said, using Mom's favorite phrase designed to heal all wounds – physical and emotional – as we grew up. It seemed to work then, so I was confident it would work now.

Chapter 63

Before we left to go back to the city, Angel went over and picked up the piece of plywood with the "swoosh" cut into it.

"You might need this for evidence at some point," he said. When we got to the car, he opened the hatch and placed it carefully inside.

As we started down the mountain, I looked over my shoulder at our backseat passengers. Angel had his arm around Nick, who rested his head on his big brother's shoulder. When Angel put a pointer finger in front of his lips, I got the hint to keep quiet and let Nick nap a while after his very unhappy visit to the treehouse. Andy put some soothing music on his car-holo and we rode home without conversation.

I wasn't talking during our ride, but I *was* thinking... a lot. I was trying to come to terms with the fact that my best friend and Team Co-Leader would be GONE in two days. That in itself was bad enough! But what the future would bring once that happened... Well, I just didn't know. It was obvious that the Team had to be informed, but how and when? Holo-texting something this devastating for Team members was out of the question. Calling an emergency meeting for later that day wouldn't work, either, since people had tickets with their families for the last performance of Kayla and Juli's play. The only day between now and the Williamsons' departure was Sunday, and we have always had a sort of unwritten agreement that only routine surveillance shifts and critical emergencies would ever take place on "Family Day."

I kept going over and over the situation in my mind, making no progress toward a solution that made sense or had any possibility of working. By the time Andy pulled into the Williamsons' driveway, nice and slowly this time, I had a raging headache and I had come to the conclusion that no solution existed.

Then Angel woke up Nick and the two of them climbed out of the car. Nick came around to the passenger side and gestured to me to open my window. I figured that this would be our final goodbye, but Nick surprised me.

"So…" he began, "I guess we can tell everybody what's happening Monday morning. Dad said we're not leaving town until after he finishes some things at the office, so probably not until after noon. Do you want to call the meeting, Daniel, or should I ask Elliott to schedule it?"

I breathed a huge sigh of relief. "Let's schedule it through Elliott for 9 am. It'll be easier for us both. I'll holo him on the way to our house."

Then the enormity of what was happening suddenly hit me. As Nick was turning away toward his house, I stopped him. "Nick, wait!" I called, climbing out of the car and catching up to him. I flung myself around him in a huge bear hug and held on tight. He hugged me back and we just stood there together, not embarrassed in the slightest to be showing anyone watching that our brotherly affection for each other was real and strong.

Andy got out of the car to shake hands with Angel, a handshake that evolved into a hug of its own. Our two older brothers came over to us, patting our backs in a kindly "Break it up" signal.

"Let's go, Daniel," Andy said, walking over to the driver's side. Angel gave a back-hand wave as he ushered his brother toward their front door. Nick looked over his shoulder.

"See you Monday," he said. It sounded like any other ordinary goodbye, but I knew it wasn't.

On most Sundays, I usually slept in a little later, but I always had some activity planned that would get me out of the house. About four times a year I visited the Las Vegas Natural History Museum to see how their Dinosaur Exhibit had expanded. (There was always something new!) Sometimes I went to the Shan-Gri-La Prehistoric Park just to hang out with people who like dinosaurs. It was fun for me to hear how many little kids said they wished they were dinosaurs. If there was a new movie to see, I would often call up Nick and Lynnelle (our movie guru) to take in a matinee with me.

On this particular Sunday, my third usual option – the movie with Nick – was a no-go, and, to tell the truth, I simply had no energy or interest for doing… ANYTHING. I was still in bed at 12:30 when Dad opened my door quietly, poked his head in and asked if I was all right.

"Yeah, I'm ok. Just upset, I guess," I said.

He came in and sat on the corner of my bed. "Upset? Why?"

So I told him what was going on with the Williamsons' move and how disappointed I was that Nick waited until yesterday to tell me about it.

"Maybe he figured that if he didn't tell *you,* it wouldn't actually happen," Dad said. "It sounds to me like neither Nick nor Angel *wants* to move to New Jersey, but kids don't always have a say in these things."

"Maybe," I said. "The whole thing sucks, though."

"Look at it this way," Dad suggested. "You have been best friends for years, and there's no reason that a little distance will change that. You and Nick have the same kind of friendship that Rob and I have. He lives in New Jersey, too, and we only get to see each other every five years or so, but we keep in touch all the time and we are still BEST FRIENDS after twenty years! Nick will be only a plane ride away. You two just need to commit to keeping your friendship the same, despite the miles separating you."

What Dad said made sense. More important, it pulled me out of my depression and gave me a Plan of Action that would begin Monday.

Dad got up and leaned over to give me a hug. "All better?" he asked with a wink.

"All better!" I said, smiling at our always-appropriate family saying.

After Dad left, I got busy making the "All better" situation a reality. I contacted Elliott on a private link and gave him his instructions for Monday. Then I got up, showered and headed for the Natural History Museum. (Three miles each way was perfect exercise for a Sunday!)

When I woke up Monday at 7 am, Elliott's message was on my wall screen, waiting:

THE STAGE IS SET, DANIEL. HAVE A GOOD DAY!

I took a really long shower and spent more time than usual on my hair and teeth... not exactly putting off leaving for Headquarters, but maybe because I still had a glimmer of hope that today's meeting would become unnecessary because a miracle had occurred in the Williamson household since Saturday afternoon.

Dad had apparently told Mom what was going on, because she had prepared a breakfast for me of two waffles with blueberries, three eggs over-easy, a piece of buttered cinnamon-raisin toast and FOUR sausages (two more than usual). A 16-ounce glass of orange juice replaced my customary glass half that size.

"Gosh, Mom!" I said, sitting at the table. "Why such a huge breakfast?"

"Your Dad felt you might need extra energy this morning. A good breakfast is always the best start for a good day!" she said. "Eat up!" And she left the kitchen with a breakfast tray for Xander.

I turned on the wall screen to catch up on local news as I ate. The morning News Anchor was just introducing my favorite "HMMMMM" segment, which always covered some local mystery or situation to make people wonder – until the mystery was solved, that is. The *SpinoRex* attack in the Northwest section of the town last year was a "HMMMMM" segment until the attack on Molasky cleared up that mystery.

Today the "HMMMMM" reporter, Marilyn Flynn, began her segment standing on a path in front of a forest that looked familiar to me. She walked down the path, talking over her shoulder, as her cameraman followed.

"Viewers, we have a real mystery here today. The Park Ranger contacted Action News late yesterday to report some substantial damage to a particular area of this pristine forest – damage that he said could not have been weather-related or the result of indigenous wildlife activity. Let's have a look."

She tiptoed gingerly along in her high-heels. The Steady-Cam behind her kept her in frame as the clearing where Nick and Angel's treehouse used to be came into view. The camera panned the scene to take in the full scope of the destruction.

Marilyn positioned herself in front of the biggest debris pile, gesturing as she spoke. "You can see here piles of broken siding, smashed framing and shattered shingles that USED TO BE a much-beloved, hand-built treehouse that had stood on this spot for more than thirty years, according to Ranger Henry O'Shea."

The feed cut to a recorded holo with the Park Ranger.

"Yes, we in the Park Service have known about this treehouse for many years, and although people are not usually allowed to build on Park land, we know that it was a couple of kids who have added to the original treehouse over the last few years, so we let it pass." He looked off to his left, then went on. "No, ma'am… no local animals did this," he said. "It is obvious that this destruction was PERSONAL." He looked again to his left. "How do I know it was personal? Well, until Saturday afternoon there was a piece of plywood over there with a large symbol carved in it. The plywood is gone now, but I know I saw it. Whoever has that piece of plywood should turn it over to Metro, in my opinion."

The feed cut back to Marilyn. "Thank you, Ranger O'Shea. So, viewers, we have to say 'HMMMMM' to this Treehouse Destruction in the public forest here on Mount Charleston and to the unexplained mark on a piece of missing plywood. Stay tuned for updates on this latest mystery. This is Marilyn Flynn reporting. Back to you in the studio."

The screen faded to "rest" mode but I sat there staring at it. *How did* **Action News** *find out about the wrecked treehouse?* I wondered. *Did Ranger O'Shea call the TV station after we left there Saturday? Who <u>else</u> could have told them about it? And the ranger actually SAW the plywood that now resides in the back of Andy's car. What should we do about <u>that</u>?*

It's moments like these when I need to talk with my Co-Leader Nick and get his perspective. Oh wait… I won't have a Co-Leader after noon today. I AM ON MY OWN. Rats!

Sebastian came into the kitchen as I cleared the table, rinsed my plate, glass and silverware and put them in the dishwasher. As I picked up my jacket in the family room, Dad called out from the living room, "You guys ready?"

"Coming!" I called, walking to meet him at the front door, not actually sure I was "ready" at all for this day.

Chapter 66

I have to say that Elliott outdid himself in preparations for the Monday morning activity at Headquarters. As we Team members arrived, each of us discovered a "Sit here" or "Stand here" sign with our name on it. We looked at each other in confusion at first, but most of us were so used to being ordered around by Elliott that no one thought to ask "Why?" I was a little surprised that Sebastian's name was on a "Stand here" poster, though, since all the other assignments were for Team members – and he wasn't one... not yet, anyway – but I was glad that he had tagged along with me. By 8:55 only two assigned spots remained unfilled.

"Where are Nick and Angel?" Timeer asked, looking at me.

"They'll be here in a minute," I said, hoping I was telling the truth.

We waited in silence for a few minutes, with most of us covering our uneasiness by checking our holos every few seconds. None of us were receiving any messages, though... which was a little unusual.

When I saw the conference room door open, I looked up. Nick and Angel entered, smiled just a bit at us and took their assigned spots, both of them obviously "in on" Elliott's plan. Immediately, the large screen opposite us came to life and Elliott spoke:

"EVERYONE, THIS IS OUR FIRST ANNUAL TEAM PHOTO SESSION. LOOK THIS WAY, PLEASE, AND... SMILE!"

Sebastian put up a hand and stepped away from his assigned spot.

"I'm not a Team member," he told the unseen Elliott. "I don't belong in this photo."

"STEP BACK TO YOUR SPOT, MR. MONTGOMERY," Elliott intoned. "YOU ARE TO BE IN THIS PICTURE. PERIOD."

Sebastian jumped a little at Elliott's booming tone, but slid back into his assigned spot next to Johnny.

"AS I SAID, **SMILE!**" Elliott boomed again, and we all followed directions. About twenty rapid-fire flashes ensued before Elliott was satisfied and he "dismissed us" to begin our meeting. We all took our usual seats around the conference table, and I pulled up an extra chair next to me for Sebastian. Nearly everyone was looking at me, since I usually led our meetings, but it was Angel who spoke first.

"Hey, everyone," he said. "Sorry we were a little late. And thanks for going along with our surprise photo session. It was something my brother and I really wanted to do today."

He looked at Nick. "Ready?" Nick shook his head no.

"Do you want me to tell them?" Angel asked. Nick nodded once and looked down at his feet. Then he suddenly raised his head and looked at his brother.

"No, I'll tell them," he said. Angel patted his shoulder and pushed his chair back from the table a little.

Nick closed his eyes. Summoning courage? Trying to choose the right words? It was quiet in the room, really quiet. Finally, he opened his eyes and took a deep breath.

"After a wonderful year of being your Co-leader of Team Triassic and Angel being a great Team fighter, I'm heartbroken to say that Angel and I are leaving the Team today."

Kayla gasped. Johnny cried, NO!" Everyone looked at each other in disbelief.

"WHY?" Matthew shouted, jumping up out of his seat. "WHY?"

Angel moved forward. He looked at his brother, who nodded, then he explained what Andy and I already knew but what I was still not willing to believe.

"The only reason we are both stepping down from Team Triassic is because our family is moving from Las Vegas to Southern New Jersey... TODAY."

"WHAT!?!" Everybody around the table said almost in sync. Then there was commotion all around the room as people cried out, "Why didn't you tell us?" "Why *today?*" "You CAN'T just leave!" "We NEED you both!" and every other sort of cry of distress. "Who's going to be my pranking buddy now?" Lynnelle cried, tears streaming down her face.

Nick cleared his throat and tried to speak. His voice cracked with emotion as he said, "I would've told you all sooner, but I couldn't. Every time I thought about it, it would make me upset, and I was really hoping that it wasn't going to happen. We don't want to leave you guys." He choked up, unable to go on.

"Why are you moving?" Matthew asked. "Don't your parents like Las Vegas?"

"It's not that," Nick sighed. "My Mom got a job there... with her college roommate, who owns a very successful design business. At first, Mom thought she could do designing from here, but that isn't going to work. And when Dad also got a great job offer in New Jersey... Well, there was no way they could say no. Mom and Dad decided that we have to move."

"Will you be coming back... to visit, at least?" Juli asked, dabbing at her eyes with a tissue.

"You bet!" Angel said. "We'll be only a couple of thousand miles away!"

His chrono chimed then and he said, "Nick, we have to go." Nick hesitated, but Angel put an arm around his back to urge him to stand up. Everybody took that as a signal to get up, too, and arrange themselves into a sort of "reverse receiving line" to say their goodbyes. Andy and I stayed back.

Lynnelle walked up to Nick and gave him a big hug. "I'm going to miss you so much, Nick," she said, sobbing into his chest.

"I'll miss you, too, Prank-Buddy. I'll text you and holo you, I promise," Nick said. Lynnelle gave Angel a hug and went to wait by the door.

Juli walked up to both Angel and Nick and pulled them into a hug together. "We all love you both. Your spirits will live on here... until you come back to us," she said.

Timeer gave Nick and Angel individual "bro hugs." Breaking away, he said, "I'm going to miss both of you, Dudes. You are a great leader, Nick. Be safe."

"I'll miss your energy a lot. You stay safe here, too," Nick said.

As the rest of the Team came forward to say their individual goodbyes, I ducked out to our office to grab my jacket. To my surprise, there was a beautifully wrapped present in the center of my desk blotter. The card said, "To my Best Friend, Daniel."

I opened the box. Inside was an antique golden pocket watch. I turned the watch over to read the engraving: To my Other Brother. There will never be a TIME we'll be apart. NICK Inside a bright orange sleeve next to the watch was a flashdrive with a cover marked "T T: IMPORTANT. I tucked the watch into my right pocket and the flashdrive into my left.

I got back to the conference room just as Johnny, last in line, was doing his best to keep it together. When he stepped up to Nick, he covered his face with his hands, speechless for a moment.

"Hey, it's ok. We'll see you again soon, Johnny," Nick said.

Johnny hugged Nick. "You guyth better not thay it if you don't mean it!" he said.

"We mean it, Johnny," Angel said, patting him on the back. Johnny nodded, but he didn't look very convinced as he walked out the door and headed to the Control Room.

Then it was just me, standing there with Nick and Angel. I felt like my feet were rooted to the floor. Somehow it seemed that if I stayed perfectly still in this conference room, maybe time would stop and my friends wouldn't leave. Nick and Angel weren't moving, either. Maybe they felt the same way.

A loud BANG on the door jamb broke me out of my inertia. It was Andy, poking his head around the open door. "Yo, you guys! Get a move on. You have a plane to catch!"

Nick and Angel sprang into action, grabbing their backpacks. I just stood there.

"Come ON, Bro!" Andy shouted at me. "Dad's waiting to drive you and me to the airport. We'll get lunch that new View Patio and then watch their plane take off. A last chance to wave goodbye... ok?"

"OK!" I said, happy that the end was not here... yet.

Exiting the gate, we saw Mr. Williamson leaning against the passenger door of his Audi, chatting with Dad. When they saw us, Mr. Williamson handed Dad a pack of papers and the two men shook hands. Angel and

Nick climbed into the Audi's back seat. When Angel rolled down the window, I realized they probably wanted to say something, but I turned away quickly in an effort (futile) to keep my emotions in check. Employing a bit of "theater," I combined a backward wave with a quick swipe across my tear-stained cheeks, hoping no one noticed the latter.

Mr. Williamson walked around to the driver's side, revealing Mrs. Williamson sitting in the passenger seat. The handkerchief she was holding in front of her face was wet with tears.

Dad and I climbed into our front seat and Andy stretched out across the backseat. All of us were quiet as we followed the Williamsons down the mountain toward McCarran.

About halfway to the airport, I leaned over to peek at the papers Dad had placed on the console.

"Why did Mr. Williamson give you the title to their Audi?" I asked Dad, breaking the silence.

"Hmmh?" Dad responded, obviously not hearing my question as he concentrated on Vegas driving.

"The papers?" I asked, picking them up.

"Oh yes," Dad said, leaning over to say, "They asked me to sell their Audi, since they're driving a rental U-Haul van to New Jersey, which means they won't be using the Audi after today, and I know somebody who wants it." He stopped a moment, then added, "Unless I should keep it for you. What do you say?"

"Dad, I'm only 15," I said. "I have a year to go before I can even get a permit!"

Dad seemed to drop the subject, concentrating on the busy traffic. I watched the passing cars for a few minutes, then asked, "Why are they driving a rental van? Aren't they having their furniture moved by Atlas or some other van line?"

Keeping his eyes on the road, Dad explained the situation. "Well, I understand that Mrs. Williamson has some very precious treasures – heirlooms from her family, mostly – that she didn't feel comfortable trusting to a moving company. She packed them all herself – Nick's Dad says they should have bought stock in a bubble-wrap company – and she made special arrangements for the boys to fly to Philadelphia today. Mrs. Williamson's friend Clara will pick the guys up and get them settled at the B & B in Newfield where the family will stay while they're house-hunting. This plan will let Nick enroll at Buena Regional in time to start school next Monday. The Williamsons and their U-Haul van should arrive in Newfield by about then, too. But the boys will be on their own for a week."

"Wow," I said, trying to take it all in. "I thought they were all flying out of McCarran today."

"Nope!" Dad said simply. "Just Nick and Angel. And you are seeing them off." He turned into Airport Drive and followed signs to the parking garage.

As he pulled into a spot on M-level and put the gear in "Park," he turned to me. "So...you can get your permit a year from now?"

"Yeah…" I said, wondering why that subject was resurfacing.

He smiled widely. "Well, I guess that means you need to put 'Driving lessons with Dad' on your calendar for … say, one year from today?"

"OK," I said, amused at the prospect of scheduling a driving lesson *a year* in advance. But mostly, I was glad that Dad seemed to *want* to spend this one-on-one quality time with me. When you have a Dad who is always so busy with one super-important project after another, every chance to spend time alone with him is precious. Now I just need to find a calendar for the year after next to "pencil us in!"

Since Dad had arranged to pick up the Williamsons' Audi at the parking garage, we stopped by our house on the way to the airport to switch to Andy's car. In what was obviously a pre-planned arrangement, Dad directed Andy to drive to the M-Level, where he pulled in next to the Audi.

"I'll leave you here," Dad told Andy and me as we got out of the car. "I have the Audi's extra keys." He climbed into the Audi and headed toward the spiral exit ramp, waving at us from the car window.

The Williamsons were probably already checking the guys in for the flight to Philadelphia, so Andy and I made our way to the brand-new View Patio. This recent addition to McCarran – open to travelers and airport visitors alike — contains a full Food Court and over fifty tables positioned around its glass perimeter, providing perfect sightlines to most of the commercial runways. The Patio is a recent addition to the airport, probably the idea of a grown-up who had spent lots of hours as a kid parked head-in to the fence on Paradise Road, where Las Vegans had watched planes taking off and landing for decades. What I remember about Paradise Road is that its popularity and limited space meant we could never find a parking place anytime we wanted to watch planes. So I am really happy with the View Patio!

Andy and I had plenty of time to stand in the View Patio's long food line, get our Double Burger & Fries (Andy) and Carne Quesadilla (me), each with a super-sized Dr. Pepper, gobble down our lunch and even go back for dessert while we waited, keeping an eye on updates for Flight 478 on the overhead monitor. We were just returning from offloading our second pile of trash when we were surprised to see Nick and Angel come into the patio from the Departures lounge. They hurried over to us, dropping their carry-ons when they were close.

Breathlessly, Nick said, "Bro, we couldn't leave without this!" He grabbed me in a tight hug.

I wrapped my arms around him and held on. *Maybe if I don't let go, he won't leave,* I said to myself. But reality settled in, as I knew they still had to get through Security, so when Nick released his hold on me, I let go, too. Angel and Andy had already finished their one-arm hug, so I stepped to Angel for a one-arm hug of my own. Nick grabbed onto Andy and said something in his ear. Andy nodded, then Nick and Angel stepped back, picked up their carry-ons, and turned toward the Departures lounge entrance.

"See you soon!" I called, hoping it was true.

"Yeah, see you, guys!" Angel called over his shoulder. Nick just gave a backward wave as he went through the door.

Two more desserts and another 45 minutes later, the monitor let us know it was takeoff time. Andy and I walked together to the Runway 7R overlook. I guess my brother realized that the next few minutes were going to be hard for me. He came close, threw his arm around my shoulder and said, "Bro, Nick asked me to remind you of something."

I looked at him. "What?"

"He wants you never to forget: 'You will always be brothers.'"

"I hope so," I said. "I miss him so much already."

Chapter 69

As Flight 478 raced down the runway, I could see somebody waving from a window seat about a third of the way back, where Economy Plus would be.

"That *has* to be Nick," I told Andy, doing my best to convince myself, too. "He said they had upgraded coach seats." Andy and I each waved wildly with both hands, expecting that *somebody* in that window seat would appreciate our enthusiastic farewell, even if it wasn't Nick.

Then a VERY amazing thing happened. As the plane left the ground and soared toward cruising altitude over Lone Mountain, a *rainbow* appeared above it, curving just high enough for the aircraft to pass between its colorful arch and the mountain top. As the plane disappeared into the clouds, the rainbow's colors intensified over Lone Mountain, its reverse reflection shining brightly in the windows of Dad's mountain laboratory, creating a perfect circle of the color spectrum.

It was so beautiful! And I had to believe that this was some kind of "sign" that things were going to be ok for Nick and me. We truly will "never be apart." He is now and will always be "my other brother."

As we walked back to Level M of the parking garage, I was feeling pretty good about life in general. When we got to Andy's car next to the now-empty Audi space, he climbed in behind the wheel. I walked around to the passenger side and saw there was a note tucked under the wiper blade. I grabbed it and opened it.

In Nick's unmistakable handwriting, it said: "STOP AT THE OFFICE ON YOUR WAY HOME."

I know the note wasn't there when we left the car here earlier. How did it get here? I held it out for Andy to see and he smiled.

"OK, Bro, a side-trip it is!" Andy generally loved the opportunity to drive, so he was one happy guy for the next 30 minutes. The two of us kept time to the Classic Rock music on his car's holo until he pulled up to the front gate at Lone Mountain, where he shifted into "Park" with a flourish, cracked open two windows but turned up the heat, put in his earbuds and reclined his seat.

"I'll wait out here for you," he shouted over the booming rock music on his holo.

I got out and waved at him as I went through the gate. *Why does Nick want me to make another stop here today?* I wondered, as I headed into Headquarters.

Chapter 70

When I opened my office door, I could see immediately that my usually not-so-tidy desk had been cleared of everything except for my desk holo and one other item, propped up against it, facing the window. I walked around the desk.

In front of me then was a framed picture of Nick and me. But this was not just any picture. It was the shot that Andy took of the two of us on the day I was released from the hospital last year. I was in the hospital's wheelchair and Nick was crouched down so he could wrap his left arm around my shoulders. Our two right hands were clasped firmly together, and we looked at each other with… well, with COMPLETE HAPPINESS.

I remembered that moment as though it was yesterday. It was when I knew that our friendship – Nick's and mine – would be lifelong.

"Boy, I really needed to see this today," I said out loud… to no one. I pulled out the frame's backboard and positioned the picture on the left corner of my desk, where I would see it every day – no matter *what* was the condition of the rest of my desktop. Whatever my future might hold, I was now absolutely sure that somehow Nick would be part of it.

"Bro – you ok?"

It was Andy at my office doorway.

"I thought you were waiting in the car," I said.

"Decided to save gas, so I came to find you. And to bring this." He held up the piece of wood from the treehouse with the carved marking.

When he turned it around a little to hand it to me, suddenly the curved groove no longer looked like a "swoosh." It looked… "OMG!" I said. "It's a J!"

Andy looked closely. "Bro, I think you may be onto something," he said. "Do you think it's…?"

We looked steadily at each other, but neither of us wanted to say what we were both thinking. After a few very long seconds, Andy sighed, breaking our silence, and summed things up perfectly:

"Looks like there's going to be some work ahead for Team Triassic," he said. He handed me the piece of wood and threw his arm around my shoulder.

"Looks like it," I said. "We'd better get to it!"

DINOSAURS WITH HUMAN HYBRIDS
IN TEAM TRIASSIC, BOOK 2

CHARACTER	HUMAN DINO HYBRID	SIZE, FEATURES	ABILITIES, TALENTS
Lynnelle	Ankylosaurus	12' long Armored body Club-like tail Low to the ground	Great at surveillance & guidance
Kayla	Apatoaurus	30' or longer Long neck Strong forelimbs Whip-like tail	Intimidating size Head height is great for surveillance

Johnny	 **Ostafrikasaurus**	18' long Large, thick teeth Concave cranium	Endurance Loud roar Excellent pack animal
Michael	 **Velociraptor**	6', bird-like Feathered but flightless Deadly talons	SPEED Fearless Often underestimated
Matthew (new) *Velociospinus*	 **Spinosaurus+ Velociraptor**	Hybrid 12' tall *Velociraptor* claws Plates near neck Smaller sail along spine than on Spinosaurus hybrid Powerful, flat tail Looks more like an oversized Velociraptor	*Spinosaurus:* Good swimmer POWER Strength *Velociraptor:* SPEED & daring Deadly claws Good tracker
Timeer (new) *Volanto Crocotalus*	 **Suchomimus + Pterodon**	8' long Crocodile- like snout Strong jaws 12' wingspan	SPEED in flight Acrobatic flier Fearsome talons
Angel	 **Tyrannosaurus Rex**	20' tall Short forelimbs Deadly TEETH	Intimidating posture Strongest bite of all Fearless

Tucker	 Confuciusornus	Size of a crow Clawlike projections at mid-wing joints Dewdrop tail ends	Soars & darts to distract enemies Deadly talons
Aurora	 Triceratops	Length 26' Height 7' Weight 6-13 tons Features a huge bony crest & 3 horns Parrot-like beak	Strong Good defender, but slow-moving
Daniel & Nick (new) *Regem* *Insuprabilus*	PROPRIETARY RECIPE	22 feet tall Egg-shaped skull Oversized horns Spinal spikes	Extremely intimidating Fearless fighter Intelligent "Unbeatable"
Andy *Avian* *Sinustrodon*	PROPRIETARY RECIPE	California condor size Bat-like wings Golden feathers	Excellent tracker: Keen sense of smell SPEED in the air

NON-HYBRID MEMBERS OF TEAM TRIASSIC
Juli, Xander & Sebastian

COMING SOON...
TEAM TRIASSIC, Book 3